SMUGGLERS' BRAND

BRADFORD SCOTT

SAGEBRUSH
Large Print Westerns

First published in the United States by Pyramid Books

First Isis Edition
published 2017
by arrangement with
Golden West Literary Agency

A catalogue record for this book is available
from the British Library.

ISBN 978–1–78541–392–6 (pb)

Published by
F. A. Thorpe (Publishing)
Anstey, Leicestershire

Set by Words & Graphics Ltd.
Anstey, Leicestershire
Printed and bound in Great Britain by
T. J. International Ltd., Padstow, Cornwall

This book is printed on acid-free paper

CHAPTER
ONE

"The most murderous, thieving, God-forsaken hole in the Lone Star State, or out of it. A small village of smugglers, and other lawless men, with but few women and no ladies."

That's how a member of General Taylor's staff described it in its early days. To the last of which a prominent citizen retorted, "Ladies are all right, I reckon, but I've never seen one yet that was worth a hang as a cook!"

To all of which, judging from the reports that had been coming in of late, Ranger Walt Slade, he whom the *peons* of the Rio Grande river villages named *El Halcon* — The Hawk, was willing to subscribe as he sat Shadow, his great black horse, on the bluff and gazed down at the two-tiered town that was Corpus Christi.

From the graceful half-moon shoreline, the three distinct sections of the town swept away to the south and west. Along the waterfront were saloons, cheap hotels, dance halls and various places of "entertainment," the least said of the better. Then came the principal business district. Still farther back, overlooking the entire scene from its upward-flinging slopes was the residential section, a conglomeration of well built houses, adobes, and shacks.

Slade thought that the section was typical of the town's inhabitants. Along with prosperous and ethical business and professional men, there were tough longshoremen, sailors from all the bright water ports of the world, lawless Border dwellers, visiting cowhands, hard-eyed watchful men from the hills, chuck-line riders and individuals who had found other localities too hot to hold them.

Rolling a cigarette with the slim fingers of his left hand, Slade hooked one long leg comfortably over the saddle horn and sat gazing toward the sand hills of Mustang Island, lying on the horizon like tawny clouds, with the gray-green waters of Corpus Christi and Nueces Bays sweeping toward them in undulating curves.

Sitting his magnificent black horse, Slade made a striking picture against the blue-gold of the late evening sky. Very tall, more than six feet, the depths of his chest and the width of his shoulders matched his height. His lean, deeply bronzed face was dominated by long, black-lashed eyes of pale gray, cold eyes that nevertheless always seemed to have little devils of laughter dancing in their clear depths. His pushed-back "J.B." revealed crisp, thick black hair above a broad forehead. His mouth, rather wide, grin-quirked at the corners, relieved somewhat the sternness, almost fierceness evinced by the high-bridged nose above and the powerful chin and jaw beneath. He wore the homely but efficient garb of the rangeland — "levis,"

2

and faded blue shirt brightened by the vivid neckerchief looped at his sinewy throat, and well scuffed half-boots of softly tanned leather. About his lean waist were double cartridge belts, with the plain black butts of heavy guns protruding from carefully worked and oiled cut-out holsters. And from those black gun butts his slender, muscular hands seemed never far away. Lounging easily in the saddle, he gazed toward the distant islands without really seeing them, for his thoughts were elsewhere. Abruptly he straightened, staring.

"What in blazes!" he exclaimed aloud.

From the waterfront mushroomed a tremendous cloud of bluish smoke shot through with flashes of flame. A moment later there came to his ears the deep, rumbling roar of an explosion. It was followed almost instantly by other minor explosions.

The flashes of flame intensified. The smoke cloud spiralled into the sky, the great column widening, breaking into fantastic streamers as the high wind beat against it.

The smoke changed color from dirty blue to black, a turgid, ebon cloud rolling across the town on the wings of the wind.

"Oil!" Slade told Shadow. "Now it's going to really let go."

There was another thundering explosion, and another. As the smoke was blasted away by the concussion, Slade caught a momentary glimpse of the masts and rigging of a ship with fire running up the shrouds and ratlines.

"Thought so," he said. "Now the oil drums are letting go. But that first one wasn't an oil drum. That was an explosive of some sort or another. Funny thing to do, mix dynamite or its equivalent with an oil cargo. Horse, I reckon we'd better amble down that way and see what we can find out. Beginning to look like we're going to have a real interesting time in this pueblo before the final brand's run."

Shadow snorted his disgust with the whole affair but obediently slid down the long slope at a smooth, running walk which ate up the distance. Swaying easily in the saddle, Slade kept his eyes fixed on the waterfront conflagration that showed little sign of abating.

Slade entered the town by way of South Staple Street. Following Kinney and William Streets, he reached Water Street. At the corner was a saloon in front of which was a hitch rack. He dropped the split reins to the ground, knowing that Shadow would not stray, and hurried along Water Street to the scene of pandemonium that marked the fire. Now he could see that an old windjammer, a schooner, was wrapped in flames. Hand pumpers were pouring futile streams of water onto the fire. A dense crowd, shouting, yelling, gesticulating, seethed and eddied, bawling unheeded advice to the perspiring firemen. As Slade shoved his way through the throng a wilder yelling signalled a new and disastrous development. The hawser which moored the schooner to the wharf had parted, and the burning vessel was swinging crazily along the wharf, carried by some vagrant current.

Directly in its path was a small but smart looking pleasure craft. It struck the little boat with a crash. There was a rending and splintering and the two vessels were locked together by their own wreckage.

The mooring line of the boat ran out to full length, tightened with a hum and the two craft jerked and bobbed wildly nearly fifty feet from the shore.

"That's old man Kendal's fishing smack!" a voice shouted. "She's a goner!"

It looked that way, all right. The fire had spread to the smack and was eating its way forward. Oil spouted from the burning ship and instantly caught fire. In a matter of seconds the water surrounding the wrecks was a flicker of flames.

Slade continued to push his way forward until he was opposite the doomed ships.

"Hey! somebody's on that smack!" another voice bawled above the uproar. "Heck and blazes! it's a girl!"

Slade could see her now. She was small and slender with masses of dark, wind-tossed hair. Her face was a white blur against the rolling smoke clouds. She stood at the very tip of the bow, with the flames roaring behind her.

A storm of cries and curses arose, and horrified exclamations. "Launch a skiff!" somebody yelled. "Go get her!"

"You loco windspider!" bellowed another voice. "A skiff'd be burned to a cinder 'fore it got half way there! Can't you see the whole bay is afire?"

Slade stared at the little figure backed by the raging inferno. His gaze dropped to the dancing mooring line that was taut as a bar of steel. The mooring post was rather high and the thin cable stretched more than ten feet above the fire-flickering water. He measured the distance with his eye.

"Believe it could be done," he muttered. Another glance at the doomed girl and he was charging to the edge of the dock, flinging men right and left from his way. He gripped the line firmly and went off the wharf and along the fragile "thread," hand over hand. Behind him the crowd howled and shouted —

"You can't do it, feller!" "If that line parts you're a goner!" "Come back! Are you plumb loco?"

Slade paid them no heed. He gasped as the withering heat from the burning oil struck him. The acrid fumes made him choke and cough; but hand over hand he sped toward the tossing fishing smack with its still living cargo.

For a man of Slade's strength and agility, the trip to the boat was nothing; but what was to follow was something altogether different. He reached the side of the smack and glanced upward. The girl's eyes, wide and darkly blue, met his. There was fear in the dark eyes — only one of unsound mind would not have felt fear under such circumstances — but nothing of panic.

"Can you hear me?" he called.

"Yes, I can hear you," she answered, her voice soft, quivering a little.

"Then do just as I say," he called back. "Ease yourself over the rail and hang by your hands. Hurry!"

She obeyed, making the not easy move with lithe grace. Slade levered himself up till he had one crooked elbow over the line. He let go with the other hand and got his arm around her dangling legs.

"Easy, now," he told her. "Let go the rail. Bend forward a little and hold your body rigid."

She did so, and instantly the strain on his muscles was terrific.

"Steady!" he gasped. "Steady while I ease you down."

Inch by inch, his whole body shaking with effort, he lowered her until her face was level with his.

"Now, wrap your arms around my neck," he panted. "Hold tight, and ease yourself in behind me."

Two slender arms went around his neck and he was thankful to realize that there was muscle beneath the satiny skin. Another moment and she was behind him and he could again grip the line with both hands which was a heartening relief.

"Don't try to do anything — just hang on," he told her. "Hold tight, and don't let go, no matter what happens; if you do, it'll be curtains for us both. Hold — on!"

Twisting around, he began the terrible trip back to the wharf and safety. The strangling grip of her arms about his throat hampered his breathing. And small as was her weight, a hundred pounds or so additional strain on his arms was almost unbearable. Each time he let go with one hand to pass it over the other, he was not at all sure that he'd make it. The heat from the burning oil sapped his strength. His body was drenched with sweat. The deadly fumes choked him and seared his throat. And the wharf seemed miles distant.

The crowd had hushed and only the roar of the flames and the slapping of the water broke the stillness. On the shore men leaned forward, bent back, fingers clutching, one with the faltering hands that groped forward along the humming, vibrating line. As he suffered, they suffered with him, the breath sobbing in their throats even as it sobbed in his. In helpless agony they could only watch and wait while those hands jerked forward, tensed, held, jerked forward again.

Slade's breath could no longer get beyond the top of his lungs. His laboring heart was rising into his throat, choking him. On and on! One seared hand gripping the line, the other inching forward, tensing, holding rigid for an instant of numbing pain. Over and over, an endless treadmill of slow misery. Alternate bands of black and scarlet passed before his eyes, weaving, tossing. He tried to blink the infernal things away, but they persisted, rushing past like a country of marl extending forever. On and on, more slowly now as his strength drained away. Scant feet below the water and the fire. The wharf but a vision constantly receding into the distance.

The black bands were gaining the ascendancy. The scarlet had developed fluttery edges and were narrowing. Slade knew it was the heralding of the dank borderland of utter exhaustion. Once let the black completely submerge the red and he and his helpless burden would plummet into the caldron of flame that coiled upward in hungry expectancy. Only by sheer effort of the will was he holding on. Blast it! he'd whip the infernal thing! His strength surged to the fore —

8

the last flicker of the dying lamp! Hand over hand! Would the frightful monotony of sheer agony never cease!

Suddenly he realized that hands were gripping him, raising him. His numbed fingers lost their grasp on the line, but he was whisked upward, arms supporting him, voices bellowing in his ears. The relief from pain and effort was so great that he nearly lost consciousness. Very nearly, but not quite. His brain cleared, and his eyes. He could see faces. Men were crowding around him, thumping him on the back, trying to shake his hand. The girl clung to the other.

"Wouldn't have believed there was a man in the whole blankety-blank-blank state of Texas could have done it!" somebody whooped. "Feller, you're something out of this world!"

"Came darn near being," Slade answered, essaying a wan smile.

A roar of laughter greeted the sally, and more thumping. Slade realized he was near enough back to normal to feel pain.

"Take it easy," he begged. "I'll be black and blue."

A muffled boom sounded. The schooner spouted flame and smoke in every direction.

"There goes more oil!" somebody shouted.

The force of the explosion tore the smack free. The mooring line snapped and the little craft, caught by the current, whirled away from the wharf, listing heavily to starboard. All eyes turned to follow its progress.

"Let's get out of this," Slade suggested to the girl.

"Let's," she agreed.

CHAPTER
TWO

They wormed their way through the crowd, now intent on the sinking fishing boat, and reached the far side of the street. The girl was trembling and her piquant face was strained. The reaction was setting in. Slade shot her a glance and concluded she'd had about all she could take.

A few steps away was the door of a saloon. Slade steered for it. "How about a cup of coffee?" he suggested.

"That would be wonderful," she said.

"Yes, I think we can both stand one, steaming hot," he said. "In we go."

There was a lone bartender behind the long bar, nobody else in sight.

"Sure, I'll get you some coffee," he said. "Everybody else trailed their twine out to the fire. I couldn't be bothered by such a sputter. If they'd hightailed ahead of a grass fire up in the Panhandle like I have, they'd know what a blaze really is. Ever see one?"

"A couple," Slade admitted. "Yes, they're something to get caught by; travel faster than a good horse can gallop if there happens to be a bad wind. Wonder how that one on the ship started?"

"Hard to tell," replied the barkeep, moving toward the kitchen. "She has been loading oil for some Mexican port, I heard. Reckon some loco coot dropped a cigarette butt in the wrong place."

Slade was willing to concede that somebody dropped something in the wrong place, but he had his doubts about the cigarette. The initial explosion had not been one caused by burning oil. He steered his companion to a table and they sat down to await the coffee.

"And how did you happen to get caught in the middle?" he asked.

"I was lying down in the cabin, waiting for my father," she replied. "We'd planned to take a little cruise — he's an ardent fisherman. I guess I dozed off and the first explosion awakened me. I didn't know what it was, but I didn't get up at once. And with the cabin door shut, it didn't seem too close. I was just getting ready to leave the cabin when the other boat crashed into ours and knocked me off my feet. I hit my head against something when I fell and I imagine I was dazed for a few minutes. When I finally got on deck, it seemed there was fire all around me. I ran to the bow, intending to jump over and swim for it, and saw there was fire on the water all around the boat."

She paused and shuddered, then raised her big eyes to his. "There's no adequate way to thank you for what you did," she said, her voice quivering a little. "I won't even try, but you saved me from a very horrible death, and at the risk of your own life. When the men on the wharf saw you start going across the line, they gave you up as lost."

"There was really nothing to it," Slade deprecated the feat. "Just about the same as going hand over hand down a rope to grab and brand a calf."

"Oh, yes, quite similar," she replied dryly. "Only you were the one in danger of being 'branded,' thoroughly so."

"You did all right, yourself, and you were in just as much danger," he said. "No hysterics, no clutching me around the neck and strangling me or throwing me off balance."

For the first time he saw her smile, showing even little teeth as white as his own, and a dimple at the corner of her mouth. "A darn pretty girl," he thought to himself.

"I was too thoroughly scared to even be hysterical or do anything but exactly what you told me," she said. "Incidentally, *I* didn't have much choice in the matter. It was you who incurred the danger from your own choosing."

"Really, I didn't think about it," he said. "I just thought it wasn't right for a nice girl to be barbecued, and that something should be done. Speaking of barbecues, how about something to eat, too? I see the kitchen help are returning."

"I'm starved," she admitted frankly. "Besides, I'd like to stay here a while. My father will be frantic when he sees the fire, until he learns what really happened, and somebody will surely tell him we went in here."

"That's a notion, all right," Slade agreed. "If we went looking for him, we'd quite likely miss him. People saw us go in here and he'll be asking about you as soon as he shows up. If he saw the fire from a distance he'll be plenty bothered."

"And I expect he did," she said. "The chances are he would have been riding the trail from the east when the explosion occurred. The trail runs along the edge of the bluffs for miles and you can see the bay all the way."

"His name is Kendal, I believe?" Slade remarked. "I think I recall somebody calling out that your boat was Mr. Kendal's fishing smack."

"That's right, Clark Kendal," she replied. "I'm Gay Kendal." She looked expectant. Slade supplied his own name and she extended a slim little sun-golden hand across the table. They shook gravely, but with laughter in their eyes. Immediately, however, hers were grave.

"Those poor men on the schooner," she said, with a shudder. "I fear many of them must have been killed."

"Very likely," Slade agreed soberly. "There appeared to be no warning, no preliminary smoke or fire, so far as I could see; but I was up on the bluff when the first blast occurred. I could have missed something. I hope so."

A waiter came bustling over, still bubbling with excitement. Slade glanced at the girl, who made her desires known. Slade ordered for both of them. The blue eyes registered distinct approval.

While they were eating, the swinging doors banged open and a wild eyed man rushed in, glaring about. Gay waved her hand.

"Hello, Dad," she called. "Come on over."

The man, big, beefy, with grizzled hair and a square, big-featured face, lumbered to the table.

"You all right, honey?" he asked anxiously.

"Of course," his daughter replied composedly. "Were you worried about me?"

"Was I worried!" bawled Kendal. "I was miles down the trail when I saw that infernal schooner blow up. I knew she was moored close to the smack and figured you'd be aboard. I nearly killed my horse getting here and when I didn't see hide or hair of the smack I thought I'd pass out. Then folks told me you 'peared to be okay. Is this the young feller who packed you to shore over the mooring line?"

"Yes, this is Mr. Walt Slade," Gay answered. "Mr. Slade, this is my father, Clark Kendal."

Slade arose, towering over the massive Kendal, who thrust out a big paw.

"Son," he said heavily, "I'm mighty, mighty deep in your debt; the kind of debt there ain't no paying off."

"It was really a pleasure to be of assistance to the lady," Slade replied as they shook hands.

"Uh-huh, must have been some pleasure!" Kendal grunted. "With her hanging onto your neck and the fire blazing beneath you. Folks who told me what happened said they wouldn't have given a busted peso for either of your lives; they're still trying to figure how you did it. Anyhow, I guess you're lucky she isn't a fat gal."

"Very lucky," Slade chuckled, shooting a glance at Gay, who smiled and colored prettily. "But sit down, Mr. Kendal, and have a bite with us."

"Don't mind if I do," Kendal accepted, dropping into a chair. "Now I've got over my scare, I'm hungry."

"Dad," Gay asked, "was anybody killed by the explosion?"

14

"Heard somebody say nine men, including the captain, are missing and presumably dead," Kendal replied. "They won't know for sure until they comb all the waterfront bars to find out if some of 'em might be drunk somewhere."

"She wouldn't have carried a very large crew, from the size of her, or so I would assume," Slade remarked thoughtfully.

"That would be my notion," nodded Kendal. "Never can tell about those windjammer tramps, though. They go to all sorts of places and are sometimes mixed up in all sorts of business. Times when a big crew comes in handy."

Slade did not argue the point; such had been his experience.

Kendal's food arrived and he set to with appetite. But Slade felt that as he ate, the old man was studying him. Kendal's next remark proved him right.

"Cowhand, eh?" he stated rather than asked through a mouthful of ham and eggs.

"When I'm working at it," Slade acceded.

"Well, if you're hankering to work at it right now, there's a chore of riding waiting for you on my Tumbling K over to the east; I pay top wages," Kendal said.

"And he's a good man to work for, Mr. Slade, all the boys say so," Gay insinuated.

"Sounds interesting," Slade admitted, "but I'd like to stick around in town a few days first."

Kendal started to ask a question, evidently altered his intention and ended with a grunt. Slade read his mind and smiled.

"I was range boss for the Slash S over in the Big Bend country," he said. "The work was okay and so was

15

the man I rode for, but I got an urge to move on." He did not deem it necessary to explain that the *urge* was supplied by Captain Jim McNelty, the famous Commander of the Border Battalion, who, after Slade's chore in the Big Bend country was satisfactorily completed, needed his Lieutenant and ace-man elsewhere.

"Good!" said Kendal. "I can use you. I been running in Herefords of late to improve my stock, and those heavy-fleshed critters need more careful handling than old long-horns, of which I've still got plenty. This is real cow country, always has been and always will be, though some years back, when the business wasn't so good, a lot of the boys ran in sheep — Captain Richard King had better'n forty thousand head of woolies on his *Santa Gertrudis* spread, which was always his name for the King Ranch. My dad and me never did; we stuck by cows. Most of the others came back to cows eventually, although a mighty lot of wool went out of this section in those days; Corpus Christi was one of the largest wool markets in America. Yep, the woolies paid off, but I never did like the bleatin' nuisances. Never had the grass problem, with sheep cutting the range to pieces, in this section like they had in others, but just the same I don't like 'em."

"Folks in this section handled them properly, and sheep properly handled are no menace to grasslands," Slade interpolated.

"That's so," agreed Kendal, "but just the same I don't like 'em. Say! how the blazes did we get to talking about sheep? I'm offering you a job of cow chambermaidin', not sheep herdin'!"

"Guess we did get sort of off the trail," Slade smiled. "But I do appreciate your offer, sir, and the chances are I'll take advantage of it, after a little while."

Slade meant it, if developments in the section made it advisable for him to do so. Perhaps a mop of unruly dark hair inclined to curl and two very big and very blue eyes had something to do with his tentative decision. Which he did not mention to Clark Kendal, although the look Miss Gay gave him caused him to suspect that the young lady had read his mind aright and was not exactly displeased.

"How are conditions hereabouts?" Slade asked casually.

"Not too bad, but not too good, either," Kendal answered frankly. "We've had some widelooping of late, especially the spreads to the west of here. And over there in the brush country to the southwest of town there's quite a feud between owners there and Mexicans who have been raiding."

"Wonder where the raiders came from?" Slade remarked. "Better'n a hundred miles from here to the Rio Grande and the Border."

"Oh, there's quite a bunch of 'em that hole up over there," Kendal replied. "They slide up from the Border into the wild country. If you know the trails, you can run cows to the Border, even though it's quite a jaunt. And it's easy to smuggle contraband back and forth, for those that know the trails. Those kind of shenanigans have always gone on in this section. But here in town there's been some real trouble of late. What happened today was the worst yet, but it wasn't the first. Already

17

been a couple of fires on ships and some in waterfront buildings. Mooring lines have been cut so that some ships tied into each other with considerable damage done. Seamen have been larruped bad, and knifed. There's some kind of a row under way but nobody seems to know what it's all about, or if they know they ain't talking. What happened today was really bad."

"You think that schooner might have been deliberately set afire?"

Kendal hesitated. "I don't know," he replied. "I haven't had a chance to talk to anybody much. Maybe I'll find out something later, I'm sort of acquainted along the waterfront."

Slade nodded thoughtfully. His opinion that it might be a good notion to cultivate Clark Kendal was strengthened. He had not missed the rancher's momentary hesitation before replying to his question, and the vagueness of his answer. Might be, of course, that Kendal suddenly remembered he was talking to a complete stranger. And discussing such happenings too freely with a stranger wasn't always good policy. The happenings that, incidentally, provided the reason for Walt Slade being in Corpus Christi at the moment. He concluded it would be unwise to do any more probing for a while. He glanced at the clock over the bar.

"Well, I guess I'd better go pick up my horse," he said. "Chances are he'll be hungry, too, about now, and ready to bite my hand off if I don't show up pronto."

"Okay," Kendal nodded. "We're spending the night at the Kinney House on Leopard Street. Suppose you meet me at the hotel bar about ten o'clock, right?"

Slade glanced at Gay, whose eyes seconded the invitation. "I'll be pleased to," he accepted. "So long!"

Clark Kendal's eyes followed his tall figure to the door. "Now who and what in blazes is he?" he wondered. "Said he was a cowhand, when he was working at it; didn't say what he was when he wasn't."

His pretty daughter was apparently able to unscramble that one, for she replied without hesitation.

"No matter what he is or isn't, he's wonderful. Did you ever see a finer looking man?"

"Can't say as I ever did," Kendal admitted. "And he's a mite unusual, to put it plumb mild. I was sorta trying to feel him out, to learn something about him, and all of a sudden I realized that I was blabbin' away a hundred to the minute and he hadn't said anything."

"I've a notion others have felt the same way," his daughter remarked. In which Miss Kendal was eminently correct.

"Happen to notice his eyes?" Kendal asked.

"I thought they were very nice eyes," Gay replied.

"Uh-huh, when they want to be nice, but they seem to go through you like a greased knife, to look inside of you and see what's there, and if you're thinking something you'd rather sort of keep covered up, you get a queezy feeling the cover's stripped plumb off and he's looking it over."

Gay giggled, and for reasons known only to herself, she blushed a little.

"If that's so," she said slowly, "it might be a good idea to keep one's mind a total blank in his presence."

"Ain't easy to do, as you'll find out as you get older," her father grunted.

"I think I've already found out," she replied, very seriously.

CHAPTER
THREE

Slade was familiar with Corpus Christi and had no trouble locating a stable where Shadow would be properly cared for. After making sure all his wants were supplied, he held a short conversation with the big black, as he had a habit of doing, a habit common with men who ride much alone with only their horses for company.

"Looks like the reports Captain Jim received were not exaggerated," he told Shadow. "Appears there's an organized effort to strangle Corpus Christi's legitimate shipping, with perhaps a few nice little sidelines such as robbery and widelooping to stimulate things. I'd sure like to get the straight of that explosion and fire today. Everybody seems to think it was just the oil cargo which caught fire and blew up, but there's no doubt in my mind but that the initial blast was due to powder or some similar explosive. Which would mean that schooner was packing something which should never be shipped in conjunction with oil.

"And not to be discounted is the possibility that the explosion was deliberately set. If so, they used a tremendous amount of the stuff, especially as I'm pretty well convinced that the blast originated on the deck or in the upper hold. Otherwise it would have torn the bottom out of her and she would have sunk at once. As it was, it nearly tore her to pieces. Strange business all around. Well, we'll see, horse. Take it easy and I'll keep in touch with you."

Shadow snorted cheerful agreement and got busy on a mouthful of oats.

Corpus Christi was a busy and colorful town, especially after dark, and Slade spent some time walking the streets and giving things in general a once-over. All the saloons were doing a roaring business and those along the waterfront roared the loudest.

From the very beginning, the Bay had been the focus of activity and enterprise. Alonso Alvarez de Pineda, Spanish explorer and adventurer, while wandering around the Gulf of Mexico, sailed into the land-locked bay in 1519 and named it Corpus Christi, and, as was the custom, claimed everything in sight for his king.

Claiming was one thing, taking and holding was something else again. Some ambitious Spaniards with a yen to go places and, perhaps, in the hope of being forgotten in others, tried to set up settlements around the bay. The ferocious Karankawa Indians, and some other tribes almost as salty, looked upon such activities with disfavor and signified their dissent by roasting, sometimes alive, the newcomers and eating them. This was somewhat discouraging to even the most sanguine and the settlements failed to prosper.

Spanish ranchers who saw opportunity on the rangeland back from the bay did somewhat better. They ran in great herds, built fortified houses patterned after castles of feudal days, and dared the Kranks and their red-skinned brethren to do their darndest.

Jean LaFitte, the Gulf pirate, holed up there for a while, it is said, and left behind him tall yarns of buried treasure. Which later inspired a lot of digging, but no finding.

So things jogged along monotonously in the vicinity of Corpus Christi Bay, with Texas and Mexico both claiming the land, until, in 1839, Colonel Henry L. "Hank" Kinney of Pennsylvania showed up and coiled his twine.

Colonel Kinney was trying to forget a busted romance, or so it was said, and decided here was a good place to drown his sorrows. Not by plumping into the blue waters of the bay in the orthodox and accepted manner, but by squatting beside them and getting rich. Which he forthwith proceeded to do. If the Kranks and other Injuns didn't like it they could come looking for trouble and he'd give it to them till it ran out of their ears. The Karankawas concluded that he meant it and left the accommodating colonel severely alone.

The landlocked harbor made snug refuge for contraband cargoes. The colonel established Kinney's Trading Post, well fortified with walls of shell cement, and prospered.

As the Mexican War threatened, General Zachary Taylor dropped in for a visit, bringing with him five thousand troops and a flood of army gold, and Corpus Christi boomed. General Taylor found the town dominated by Kinney, who was all-powerful in the section, and commended him for bringing civilization to a savage land. Perhaps the good general said it with tongue in cheek, for "civilized" was something of a misnomer when applied to Corpus Christi. Everything is comparative, however, and at least the denizens of Corpus Christi did not eat the bodies of those they helped to take the Big Jump. Which was generally conceded somewhat of an improvement over the customs of the gentle original inhabitants of the region.

After a while, the general and his five thousand marched away, headed for Mexico, and enduring fame; the flood of army gold dried up, and Corpus Christi slumped a bit.

But not for long. Colonizers were importing settlers for the unpeopled lands of the south and west. The resourceful Kinney began a real estate promotion and saw to it that the vicinity got its share of the newcomers, much to the advantage of Corpus Christi. He also sent a large wagon train to open trade with El Paso and Chihuahua and thus started a spectacular period of wagon commerce between Corpus Christi and Mexico and with inland points. And to further prosper the town, the gold seekers of 1849 used Corpus Christi as an assembling point on the Southern Immigrant Route.

The Civil War didn't do Corpus Christi much damage and during the years that followed the Bay town bustled along, prosperous and turbulent. Cotton and other agricultural products were grown on the level black lands back of the town and as Walt Slade walked the streets that night the harbor teemed with shipping, the waterfront warehouses were crammed with bales,

24

crates and boxes, and he could hear the whistles of railroad trains. The redoubtable Kinney had long since passed on, but had left as an everlasting monument the two-tiered, rambunctious town beside the blue waters of the Bay.

The explosion and fire appeared to be the chief topic of conversation in the waterfront saloons; but Slade noticed that the discussions were mostly in low tones by tight groups that fell silent as he passed. Looked like the affair had exerted a subduing effect along the waterfront.

Strolling aimlessly along, he entered a big place, not too well lighted, near the corner of Water and Aubrey Streets. It was crowded, mostly by seafaring men and longshoremen, Slade judged, although there were a few cowhands present, some Mexicans in black velvet adorned with much silver, and a scattering of patrons in "store clothes," no doubt office workers in nearby establishments. He found a place at the bar and ordered a drink, which he sipped slowly while he studied the crowd.

Two men in sailor's garb, not far from where he stood, excited his interest. One had a raw red streak down the side of his face which Slade decided had been caused by a burn. The other's face also had a slightly blistered look. Both appeared ill at ease and constantly shot glances toward the swinging doors. He wondered what was bothering them, though perhaps they were just expecting a friend who was late.

Suddenly the doors swung open and two men entered, glancing around. Slade had a glimpse of glinting eyes and hard faces under low drawn hatbrims. Then his vision was blurred by gushing flame and swirling smoke. The room jumped and quivered to the roar of guns.

The two men in sailor's dress went down as if poleaxed. The killers whirled and dashed through the door.

Slade bounded across the room. He had to slow to circle a table and as he started for the door again, a huge hand clamped on his shoulder and jerked him back.

"Keep your nose outa it, feller!" a deep voice rumbled.

Slade whirled, sliding from under the gripping hand. He glimpsed a blocky red face and the big shoulders of the man who had halted him.

El Halcon hit him, with all his two hundred pounds and considerable irritation back of the blow. The big fellow shot through the air and landed on the floor with a crash that shook the building. Slade whirled again and streaked through the door.

But the momentary delay had been enough; the two killers were nowhere in sight.

Slade reentered the saloon, warily, thumbs hooked over his double cartridge belts. He was met by dead silence and staring eyes; but nobody made a threatening gesture.

The big fellow was sitting up on the floor, rubbing his jaw. He gave Slade an injured look.

"You didn't have to bust my neck," he rumbled querulously. "I was just trying to keep you out of trouble."

"Then I'm sorry," Slade replied; "but I don't like to have hands laid on me."

"You won't have mine laid on you again, you can bet your last peso on that," the other declared emphatically and fell to rubbing his jaw again. Slade's keen ears caught some of the murmurs running over the room —

"Knocked Cock Badding clean off his pins! I never saw that done before."

"Guess nobody else ever did, either."

"Must have caught Cock off balance."

"Uh-huh, he was off balance, all right. Plumb off balance the minute he was hit. As clean a knockdown as I ever saw. Who the devil is *he*?"

"Yes, I was just trying to keep you out of bad trouble," he repeated. "You wouldn't have a chance with that pair; they're killers."

"Evidently," Slade agreed dryly, glancing at the sprawled bodies which nobody had approached. He walked over to them and gazed down into the stiffened faces. Each man had a bullet hole between his glazed and staring eyes, and two in his chest. Some shooting! The light being what it was.

As Slade bent down for a closer look, Cock Badding was beside him.

"Wouldn't touch 'em if I was you," he advised. "Hawkins, who runs the joint, has sent for the marshal and the sheriff. Reckon they'll want to see 'em just as they are."

Slade nodded agreement and straightened up. "Do you know who they are?" he asked. Badding glanced around and lowered his voice.

"A couple of sailors from the Albatross, the ship that was blown up and burned today," he replied. "Managed to get off alive; looks like it didn't do 'em much good."

"Looks sort of that way," Slade conceded. "Wonder why they were killed?"

Badding shrugged his heavy shoulders. "Hard to tell, funny things have been happening along this waterfront of late," he replied evasively. "Maybe they saw something they weren't supposed to see."

Slade thought that Badding very likely had the right of it. He forebore asking further questions at the moment.

"Let's have a drink," he suggested.

"Don't mind if I do," Badding accepted. "That is if I can still swallow," he added with a grin that showed, stubby, uneven, but very white teeth. "Haven't been hit so hard since the time I sassed my mother-in-law."

"Really, I'm sorry," Slade smiled. "I guess I did it without thinking."

"Uh-huh, I reckon you do think a mite slow," Badding said with friendly sarcasm. "I was to blame myself, though; should have kept my paws off you. But I noticed you come in and knew you were a stranger here and wouldn't know what you were bucking."

"What was I bucking?" Slade asked casually.

"A mighty bad bunch," Badding replied shortly. Slade concluded that direct questioning was still not in order; maybe a few drinks would loosen the big fellow's tongue. As they sipped their second glass together, which Badding insisted on paying for, Slade tried an indirect approach.

"You work on the waterfront?" he asked.

"Guess I do," Badding answered cheerfully. "I'm a loading labor contractor for a number of piers."

"Sounds like an interesting job," Slade observed.

"It is, too darn interesting at times," Badding replied. "By the way, my name's Badding, as I reckon you know, Fred Badding, usually known as Cock Badding. I don't believe I caught your handle."

Slade supplied it and they shook hands. Badding chuckled over his glass. "I've sort of took a liking to you, Slade," he said. "Been a long time since anybody knocked me down and I kind of cotton to a feller who can. I just got a notion — you strike me as being an educated feller, even if you are a cowhand. Right?"

"I can read, write, and cipher," Slade smilingly admitted. Badding chuckled again, appreciating the joke.

Cock Badding was eminently correct in his surmise. Shortly before the death of his father, following business reverses that entailed the loss of the elder Slade's ranch, Walt Slade had graduated from a famous college of engineering, with high honors. His plan had been to take a post graduate course to round out his education and better fit him for the profession he intended to be his life's work. That, however, became impossible at the moment, and when Captain James McNelty, the Commander of the Border Battalion of the Texas Rangers, with whom Slade had worked some during summer vacations, suggested that he come into the Rangers for a while and pursue his studies in spare time, Slade agreed. Long since he had gotten as much and more than he could have expected from the postgrad. He still kept up his studies and more than once his knowledge of engineering had proven of value in the course of his Ranger duties. However, Ranger work had gotten a strong hold on him and he was loath to sever connections with the illustrious body of law enforcement officers. He was young and there was plenty of time to be an engineer; he would stick with the Rangers for a while.

Because of his practice of working under cover as much as possible and not revealing his Ranger connections, he had built up a peculiar dual reputation. Those who knew the truth considered him not only the most fearless but the ablest Ranger of them all. Others, who knew him only as El Halcon, insisted he was just a dangerous outlaw too blasted smart to get caught. Slade knew that his role as El Halcon the owlhoot laid him open to grave personal danger. On the other hand, it opened up avenues of information that would be closed to a known peace officer. Captain Jim was dubious and warned him that some trigger-happy sheriff or marshal might give him his comeuppance by mistake, but Slade shrugged that off and, Captain Jim not actually forbidding him to do so, ambled along and took his chances.

On two points all parties agreed: "The singingest man in the whole Southwest, with the fastest gun hand!"

Slade did not whole-heartedly concede the contention, but he was forced to admit that he could sing, and

30

that he was reasonably fast and accurate with his long-barrelled Colt Forty-five.

"Which brings me down to the nubbin of the ear," Cock Badding resumed. "I handle a large portion of the hiring for the various gangs and I can use a man like you. Lots of book work in the office and I don't like it and I ain't much good at it. What say you take a job with me? Will pay you a lot better'n following a cow's tail. I know, used to follow one myself but figured I could do better by myself than forty-per and chuck. What do you say?"

Slade pondered a moment; the offer was not without attractions. He had pretty well concluded that the waterfront was the focus of the trouble that was plaguing the Bay town. Working for Badding, who was evidently in the nature of being a waterfront boss as well as a labor contractor, opportunities might present. And without a doubt anyhow, here he had a chore to perform. Two cold-blooded murders had been committed in his presence, and as a law enforcement officer it was his duty to apprehend the killers.

"I've a notion I may take you up on it, and thanks," he told Badding. "I'll have to be leaving shortly — have an appointment at the Kinney House — but I'll try and drop in on you tomorrow."

"Anybody can tell you where I am," said Badding. "I'll be looking for you."

"Okay," Slade said, "we'll let it go at that."

"Here comes Sheriff Cole and one of his deputies," Badding exclaimed. "He looks to be in a bad temper.

No wonder, though, things sure have kept him hoppin'
of late."

The sheriff, long, lanky, grizzled and gray-faced, with
a drooping mustache and keen blue eyes, strode across
the room. His eyes widened as they rested on Slade's
face, widened questioningly. Slade's head moved in a
barely perceptible nod.

The sheriff's stare hardened to a glare. "So!" he
barked. "So *you're* here."

"Yep," Slade agreed. "Guess I'm not someplace
else."

"I wish to blazes you were!" the sheriff exclaimed
heartily. "I might have known it. Heard some ganglin'
hellion did the impossible today. Might have known it
was you. Well, where's the jigger *you* plugged? Must be
one around somewhere."

"Sorry," Slade replied. "They were out of sight
before I could get to the door."

"Harrumph!" snorted the sheriff. "That's unusual.
And where you are, trouble busts loose pronto. And
there's enough as it is, without El Halcon squattin'
here."

There was a turning of heads as men stared at the
almost legendary figure whose exploits, some of them
highly questionable, in the opinion of many, were the
talk of the Southwest. Behind Slade sounded Cock
Badding's startled comment —

"Whe-e-ew! And I tangled with *him!*"

The sheriff turned his attention to the bodies,
returned it to Slade.

32

"All right," he said, "just what happened? At least you can usually be depended on to see things straight. Tell me about it."

Slade told him, refraining from mentioning his tussle with Cock Badding. The sheriff listened in silence, tugging his mustache.

"And they were gone when you got to the door, eh? Did you get a look at them?"

"Not much of a one," Slade admitted, adding, "But I've a notion I'd know them if I happened to run into them again."

"I don't doubt it," grunted the sheriff and proceeded to conscript a squad to pack the bodies to the coroner's office. Which matter attended to, he turned back to Slade.

"Drop in at my office later," he directed. "I want to have a talk with *you*."

Slade promised to do so. The sheriff and his impromptu "pallbearers" departed. Cock Badding gave Slade a long look.

"Offer of a job still stands," he said. Slade's voice was serious but his eyes danced with laughter.

"Sure you still wish to take a chance?" he asked.

"Huh! there's folks who'll tell you I'm taking pay under the table from every man I hire," Badding returned. "Just let a feller get ahead a mite in the world and there's plenty ready with a knife for his back. Yep. I'll take a chance. But there's something I reckon I ought to tell you 'fore you sign up with me. You may be taking a chance yourself. Very likely the word'll be passed along by somebody that you tried to horn into

33

that row tonight, and the pair who did for those two poor devils may come looking for you. Remember, *they* never had a chance. It was a snake-blooded killing, if I ever saw one."

"Yes," Slade said softly, "it was!"

Cock Badding was a hard man; they said along the waterfront that he could never get his fill of fighting. But mentally, at least, he recoiled a little from the eyes that really were not looking at him but past him — eyes the color of slaty waters under a stormy winter sky, but with little flames seeming to flicker in their depths, like to fire under smoky ice — the terrible eyes of El Halcon.

"I think," Slade said deliberately, "that I will take a chance. See you tomorrow."

With a nod he left the saloon, his glance flickering to right and left. Badding gazed after him.

"*I* think," he remarked to his whiskey glass, "that any hellions who come looking for *him* will be the ones who are taking the chance!"

34

CHAPTER
FOUR

Slade found Clark Kendal at the Kinney House bar, with him one of the strangest appearing individuals The Hawk had ever seen. His face was strikingly handsome, the features almost cameo-like in their regularity. He had crisply golden hair, though shot with gray. His eyes were pale, very clear, very critical, and very masterful. He had very broad shoulders and a chest that suggested enormous strength, but below his waist were short, bowed legs, those of a dwarf who, judging the proportions of his upper body, Nature first intended for a giant. His head came barely above the bar. And, Slade thought, there was a hint of tremendous vitality — a stunted Hercules run to depth, breadth, and, very likely, brain.

Kendal waved a cordial greeting and beckoned Slade to join him. "Hayes," he said to his companion, "this is Walt Slade, the young feller I was telling you about. Slade, shake hands with Mr. Hayes Wilfred, a particular friend of mine."

The hand Wilfred extended was long and large, with bony, spatulate fingers, and his grip was like iron.

"It's a great pleasure to know you, Mr. Slade," he said. "I heard of your heroic act in saving Mr. Kendal's daughter; the whole waterfront is still talking about it. I wish to personally congratulate you."

"Thank you," Slade replied. "It really wasn't as difficult a chore as it looked to be."

Hayes Wilfred smiled. "I am rather strong in the hands and arms myself," he observed, "but I wouldn't have cared to attempt it. I'd have had an advantage over you, however," he added with a twinkle. "My short legs would have been farther away from the oil burning on the water."

"Yes, that would have been in your favor," Slade acknowledged with a smile. "My boots got a mite warm, all right."

"I don't know what things are coming to here," Wilfred remarked soberly. "We've been having considerable trouble along the wharfs of late but nothing quite as bad as today."

"Mr. Wilfred is a ship owner," Kendal put in.

"Yes," nodded Wilfred. "I have a small fleet plying out of Corpus Christi and other ports; mostly coastwise trade. So far I haven't personally had any trouble to speak of, but I'm hardly expecting to escape. There appears to be an organized bunch of trouble makers at work, and nobody's safe."

"And you've no idea who and what are the organization and what their aims?" Slade asked casually. The dwarf shrugged his broad shoulders,

"Well, for one thing, there is a great deal of unrest south of the Rio Grande right now," he replied. "The Mexican government's new land policy is unfortunate, to put it mildly, and has created bitter resentment. And

36

gun running is lucrative, if you can get by with it. Arms and munitions can be smuggled out of Corpus Christi and other ports to some obscure landing spot on the Mexican coast, and sold at a huge profit. That means strife between rival factions, and the honest shipper is caught in the middle. But the unscrupulous will do anything for gain."

Abruptly Slade saw Wilfred's eyes flash, his mouth tighten as he glanced toward the door.

A man had just entered, a tall man, raw-boned, roughly dressed, who walked to the bar with an easy, swinging stride. There was a slight roll to his gait, however, which hinted of heaving decks. Slade deduced that he very likely had had considerable to do with the sea.

"Rance Donner," Kendal remarked.

"Yes, Rance Donner," Wilfred repeated. Again a slight shrug of the big shoulders. He turned to Slade and extended his hand.

"I'll have to be going, a busy day ahead of me tomorrow," he said. "Hope you'll see fit to stick around with us a while, Mr. Slade; we can use men like you."

"Thank you," Slade replied. "Perhaps I will."

Wilfred nodded. "Good night," he said and headed for the door, with short, jerky, but assured steps. Old Clark Kendal watched him go.

"A nice feller, Wilfred," he said. "Always cheerful despite his affliction. Always makes light of it; jokes about it like he did with you. Some fellers would be held down by being made that way, but not Hayes Wilfred. He's an up and coming feller if there ever was one. Out to make a dollar, but to make it honest. Never hear him say a bad word about anybody. Take Donner over there at the bar, the feller with the sorta reddish-yellow hair and dressed like a longshoreman. He ain't got no use for Donner, I happen to know, but he'd never say so before a stranger."

"Donner in the shipping business?" Slade asked. Kendal nodded.

"Yep, he owns some old tubs. Keeps 'em in good shape, though, and always busy." He glanced around, lowered his voice.

"Some funny stories go around about Donner," he continued. "I've heard it said he got his start as a wrecker. Used to lure ships onto the rocks over around Matagorda Bay with false beacons. Just talk, maybe, but I've heard it said. Heard too that he's done a bit of smuggling in his time, and maybe a mite of piratin' of little Mexican and Central American boats. Don't know as to that. If he did, he never got caught at it. Gather the Customs folks sort of keep an eye on him, though. But don't judge the feller by what I've been telling you. It may all be just so much sheep dip. As I said, nobody has ever caught him at anything off-color, so far as I've ever heard."

Slade nodded, and regarded Rance Donner with somewhat quickened interest.

Kendal suddenly chuckled, and regarded Slade quizzically. "Son," he said, "this makes the second time today I've been spilling my guts to you right and left, and you still haven't said anything. How in blazes do you do it?"

Slade laughed outright. "Perhaps by just being a good listener," he said.

"Maybe," Kendal conceded. "Anyhow, I guess about the hardest thing in the world for a man to do is keep his mouth shut."

Slade smiled, after he had unscrambled that one. "And most of the trouble in the world can be credited to too much talking," he replied.

"You're right, there," Kendal agreed emphatically, and fell silent for a moment.

Slade, meanwhile, was studying Rance Donner who stood at the bar sipping his drink and, Slade knew, looking over the room and its occupants in the back-bar mirror.

Donner looked to be a hard man, and very likely was. His eyes were keen and alert and appeared to be constantly roving. He had a firm mouth above a long cleft chin. His nose was straight save for a slight upward tilt to the tip, and his upper lip was a trifle long. His face was broad across the cheek bones, and the cheek bones were low. His hair was tawny; reddish rather, with glints of gold, and he wore it rather long. And, somehow, the rough careless garb of a longshoreman seemed to become him. Slade had a feeling that evening dress might also well become him. For there was something about the man that set him apart from those standing near him, some of whom also wore work clothes while others displayed conservative business attire. He concluded that Rance Donner was decidedly an individual.

Donner, his inspection of the room apparently finished, set his empty glass on the bar and departed. Slade was struck by the easy grace of his movement. Kendal followed him with his eyes and shook his head.

"Hate to see a nice looking young feller like that mixed up in skullduggery," he remarked.

"You said yourself that you don't *know* he's mixed up in anything off-color," Slade reproved gently. Kendal flushed a little.

"Guess you're right there, too," he conceded. "I should tighten the latigo on my jaw." He glanced at the clock over the bar.

"I'm going to hit the hay," he said. "Been a hard day. Suppose you meet us here about noon tomorrow? Gay wanted to wait up for you but she was beginning to show what she went through today and I figured she was better off in bed and sent her upstairs. I told her that her eyes were red and her nose shiny and that she'd look a lot better after a night's sleep. That took care of *her*."

Slade chuckled. "I've a notion you have a way with women, Mr. Kendal," he said.

"Oh, so-so," the rancher replied. His stern old mouth became wonderfully sweet and tender. "Anyhow, I managed to tie onto her mother," he said. "She was a lot like Gay. Thirty years we had together. 'The Lord giveth and the Lord taketh away. Blessed be the name of the Lord!' Goodnight, son."

Slade watched his retreating form, and abruptly the little devils of laughter that always seemed to dance in the depths of his cold eyes were very kindly devils indeed.

After signing up for a room, Slade left the hotel. To reach the sheriff's office he turned into a rather poorly lighted side street. On the far side of the street was a row of unlighted warehouses and shop windows which made very good mirrors. So he had no difficulty spotting the man who stealthed along beside him, steadily drawing nearer. He was not far from where he would turn a corner when from an alley mouth ahead two more men materialized. Slade watched them approach, and at the same time kept an eye on the reflection of the man behind. The pair in front were perhaps a dozen paces distant when the man behind came forward at a rush, one hand grasping some object swinging by his side.

Gauging the distance with the utmost nicety, Slade spun on his heel and hit him, his fist thudding solidly against the fellow's jaw. Down he went with a grunt. Slade whirled about, a gun in each hand. His eye caught the glint of shifted metal as the pair ahead jerked to a halt. The street rocked to the bellow of the reports.

Back and forth gushed the lances of orange flame. One of the pair slumped to the ground. A slug ripped across Slade's cheek bone and hurled him sideways with the shock; a second grained the top of his shoulder. Even as the drygulcher fell, his gun still blazing, Slade heard a strangled cry behind him. Whirling, he saw the man he had struck pitch forward on his face, twitch an instant and stiffen out. Evidently a bullet fired by his partner's dying hand had caught him dead center.

Still a trifle dizzy from shock, Slade lurched to where the two drygulchers lay and peered into their dead faces. He whistled back of his teeth. Shouts were sounding in the distance, drawing nearer, but he took time to turn the third man over on his back and give him a quick once-over. He shook his head, straightened up and raced down the street, whisked around a corner and slowed his pace. A few moments more and he neared the sheriff's office.

The office door stood open and Sheriff Cole was standing in the street, glancing about.

"Hello!" he greeted the Ranger. "Say, didn't I hear shooting somewhere around?"

"Guess you did," Slade replied. "Come in and shut the door, and lock it."

Inside the office, Slade slumped into a chair, mopping his face with a handkerchief.

"What in blazes!" exclaimed the sheriff. "You're hurt — you're all over blood!"

"Just a scratch," Slade made light of his injuries. "By the way, you won't need to look for those hellions who murdered the two sailors in the waterfront bar. They're laying in the street around the corner, peacefully waiting for you to come and pack 'em in."

CHAPTER
FIVE

Sheriff Cole swore an astounded oath. "Will you please tell me what happened?" he pleaded.

Slade told him. "A nice try," he concluded. "If it hadn't been for those unlighted windows across the street it might have succeeded. The outlaw brand always overlooks trifles."

The sheriff swore some more. "Wherever you show up, the devil busts loose and goes on a tear," he wailed. "I wish McNelty would lock you up and throw the key away!"

"If you didn't want me here, why did you write him?" Slade countered.

"I asked him for a troop of Rangers to help clean up the waterfront," the sheriff retorted. "I didn't ask him to send El Halcon to raise Hades and shove a chunk under a corner!"

"Well, before all's finished, maybe we'll be able to kick loose the chunk," Slade predicted cheerfully.

"Uh-huh, after the graveyard's full!" snorted Cole. "Now what?"

"Now I guess you'd better amble around the corner to investigate the shooting you heard and 'discover' the bodies," Slade replied. "Be sure and go through their pockets and let me know what you find, if anything. First, though, a couple of questions. What do you know about Rance Donner?"

"Not much," replied Cole. "A salty young hellion who 'pears to be making money out of those old tubs he owns. A lot of stories going around about him. Some of 'em ain't over nice."

"A lot of stories going around about El Halcon, too," Slade pointed out.

"Uh-huh, but they're different," said the sheriff. "If the yarns I've heard about Donner happen to be true, he's been mixed up in some mighty shady businesses. Wrecked ships on a stormy night mean snake-blooded killings as a side issue. And gun running to Mexico and Central America means more killings."

"Nothing has ever been proven against Donner, I gather," Slade commented.

"That's right — nothing but yarns that seem just to start without anybody knowing for sure where they started."

"I see," Slade nodded. "What about Hayes Wilfred."

"There's a real gent, that top-heavy dwarf," the sheriff answered. "He's okay, and up-and-coming. Wish we had more like him."

Slade nodded again, and threw the blood-stained handkerchief into a wastepaper basket. The sheriff hastened to fetch a clean one from a drawer.

"Sure you don't want me to plaster that gash?" he offered.

"Go get the bodies, first," Slade replied. "I expect you'll find a crowd around them. I heard yelling as I came away. I didn't care to be mixed up in what happened, just yet. Just a minute — what do you know about Fred Badding?"

"Cock Badding? A salty jigger who likes a ruckus. Otherwise okay, so far as I know. Anything else?"

"Not for the moment," Slade decided. "I'll wait for you here."

"Soap and water in the back room if you want to wash the blood off," said the sheriff. "A roll of bandage and some stickin' plaster in the drawer there. Be seeing you."

Left alone in the office, Slade took advantage of the soap and water and the medicants. The bullet cut in his cheek was really insignificant and a strip of plaster rendered it hardly noticeable, to which a mirror in the back room attested. The slice along the top of his left shoulder was also trifling; a second strip of plaster took care of that. The bullet hole in his shirt could stand a mending, but that would have to wait.

His injuries taken care of, he sat down, rolled a cigarette and gave himself over to some serious thought. Looked like Cock Badding's conjecture was sound. Somebody had noted his attempt to follow the two killers and had passed the word along to either them or somebody else who had the authority to make decisions. Why the quick try at evening up the score? His El Halcon reputation, perhaps — El Halcon, who made a habit, or so it was said, of horning in on good things somebody else had started and skimming off the cream. Yes, that was very probably the answer. Of course, it could have been intended for a little gentle

45

hint to others to mind their own business or pay. He had already concluded that somebody was instigating a reign of terror along the Corpus Christi waterfront, an old outlaw method: scare people into keeping their eyes closed and their mouths shut. That also could be the answer.

In either case, Ranger Walt Slade was pleased. Easier to have the hellions come to him than to have to root them out. The obvious fact that the situation boded grave personal danger for himself he passed over as of little consequence. He had a chore to do in Corpus Christi and its environs; that was of primal importance.

Steps sounded outside, and loud voices. A moment later the sheriff entered, with him nearly a dozen men who packed the bodies of the three drygulchers.

"Put em in the back room," directed the sheriff. "The coroner can look 'em over tomorror. We're getting quite a collection. Thanks, boys, for lending a hand."

After a few words of conversation, the bearers filed out, casting curious glances at Slade, some nodding to him, but asking no questions.

After shutting and locking the door, Sheriff Cole turned to Slade and chuckled.

"Things worked out sort of nice," he said. "The way the hellions were laying, it looked plumb like they'd gunned each other. That's what everybody decided right off."

"That helps," Slade conceded. "Now let's give them a once-over. Did anybody recognize them?"

"The one laying by himself, yes," replied the sheriff. "Seems he was a sort of dock hanger-on. A kind of a plug-ugly down there. Never worked much but always seemed to have plenty of money. Several of the boys remembered seeing him. The other two nobody could remember anything about. Mean looking cusses, all three of 'em."

The pockets of the dead men revealed nothing of significance save a rather large sum of money.

"Been doing purty well with their skullduggery," grunted Cole, popping the bills and coin into his desk drawer. "Notice anything worth while?"

"Yes," Slade replied. "The pair who killed the sailors — look at their feet."

"Riding boots, not work shoes!" exclaimed the sheriff. Slade nodded and proceeded to carefully examine the hands of the pair.

"They've been cowhands," he announced. "Haven't worked at it for quite a while, but the marks of rope and branding iron are still discernible; if you look close. The boots clinches it. Two things a cowboy always tries to hang onto, his saddle and his boots. You know about the ornriest thing that can be said of a waddie is that he sold his saddle. And take his boots away from him and he feels undressed. Another of the little slips the owlhoot brand always makes. This is interesting."

"But what does it mean?" asked the sheriff.

"It means," Slade replied, "that they were a couple of hired killers brought in to do a chore; they did it. Knew their business, too. It was all over in that saloon before you could draw a breath. Each one fired three shots and each shot dotted the 'i.' They were sure no snides at gun slinging. Cold, nerveless, snake-blooded."

"They don't look so much," grunted Cole. "Ordinary cowhand type, I'd say. Nothing to mark 'em as killers, so far as I can see."

"There is no such thing as a criminal physiognomy," Slade said. "A man may look like a saint and be a devil, and vice versa. Some of our most ruthlesss outlaws and killers appeared anything but what they really were. Lots of folks took John Wesley Hardin for a minister. Sam Bass was just a rollicking cowhand, so far as appearances went. Doc Holliday was a sprightly, well spoke gentleman, on the surface. John Ringo could have passed for a college professor, both in appearance and the manner in which he expressed himself. Put a wart on the end of a jigger's nose, a cast in one eye, and give him buck teeth and immediately too many folks put him down as an off-color character. Just as much sense in concluding that a hombre is a firebug because he has red hair. Yes, there is nothing particularly outstanding about that pair, but they were a long way from being ordinary. And wait till this mess is cleaned up and we drop a loop on the hellion really responsible and he will possibly be the surprise of your life."

"I'm not so sure about that," the sheriff observed sententiously, "but we'll see."

"Don't go looking sideways at Rance Donner till you have a more concrete reason than gossip for doing so," Slade counselled.

"I didn't mention Donner," growled Cole.

"That's right, you didn't," Slade conceded, with a smile. "Well, I'm going to bed. The day has been a mite hectic. I'll drop in and see you tomorrow. Today, rather. It's past midnight."

"Okay," said the sheriff. "By the way, I played it right in that waterfront bar, didn't I? I gathered you wanted me to sound off about El Halcon. Right?"

"Right," Slade repeated. "I thought it would be a good notion; might cause some jigger to tip his hand."

"Or tip you back on your heels," growled Cole. "You'll get it some day, letting those El Halcon yarns buzz around and doing nothing to disprove them. A wonder McNelty hasn't put a stop to your pretending to be an owlhoot too smart to get caught."

"I didn't start it," Slade defended. "It's sort of like Topsy in Uncle Tom's Cabin, 'wasn't born, just growed.' I can't work undercover as I often do, without revealing my Ranger connections, and not have yarns start about me. Captain Jim fusses now and then, but he is forced to admit that it opens up avenues of information that would be closed to a known peace officer, and causes hellions to take chances they wouldn't take with a known Ranger. Has paid off well more than once."

"Guess that's so," the sheriff admitted, "but you're always taking the chance of some marshal or deputy plugging you on general principles. To say nothing of some gun slinger out to get a reputation by downing the notorious El Halcon, and not past shooting you in the back to get it."

"Hasn't happened so far," Slade replied blithely. "Good night."

CHAPTER
SIX

Despite the lateness of the hour when he finally got to bed, Slade was up before mid-morning. He enjoyed a leisurely breakfast at a quiet restaurant and then repaired to the waterfront. An obliging dock worker directed him to Cock Badding's office.

"Ain't you the feller who knocked Cock on his ear last night?" he asked with a grin.

"I guess he sort of slipped," Slade smilingly replied. The longshoreman guffawed loudly.

"Some slip!" he chortled. "Feller, if you ever want somebody killed and ground into sausage meat, or a church burned down, or some other little thing, all you have to do is to go to Cock Badding. Cock loves a man who can lick him, and he sure ain't had to love many. There's the office, right ahead. Reckon you'll find him in this time of day. He won't have gone out on the piers yet."

Badding was in. He greeted Slade cordially, then shot him a rather strange look.

"Understand two hellions were picked up on the street last night, shot full of holes, and another sidewinder I rec'lect with 'em. Everybody figures they got into a row and gunned each other. But I just wonder!"

"Okay, just so you don't wonder out loud," Slade answered. Badding nodded his shaggy head.

"Thought so," he said. "The two devils who killed those poor sailors, I'd say. Didn't get much of a look at 'em in the bar last night, but I'm pretty sure they were the ones. Uh-huh, remember that I told you last night, that you might have started trouble for yourself. Oh, well, I've a notion you can finish any you start, so we won't pay it any mind. Going to sign up with me?"

"If you still want me after — what has happened of late," Slade replied.

"Sure I want you," growled Badding. "When can you start?"

"Tomorrow be okay?" Slade asked. "I have an appointment with Clark Kendal for noon today."

"A good man, Kendal," nodded Badding. "Sure tomorrow will be okay. I'll be looking for you. Don't take any chances you don't have to take. There's such a thing as a feller playing his luck too strong, you know."

"I'll try and play 'em close to my vest," Slade promised.

"You won't, but I've a notion that when the showdown comes, you'll have aces back-to-back," Badding predicted cheerfully. "Be seeing you!"

Slade walked around the waterfront for a while, then headed for the Kinney House. He found Clark Kendal and Gay awaiting him in the lobby.

"First off, let's have something to eat," the rancher suggested. "Then how about ambling down to the waterfront with us? I was out early and bought another boat; she's a beauty, a lot better than the one I lost. Gay likes to sail and I wouldn't want her to be disappointed. You can look the craft over and then you two can try her out. Okay?"

"Suits me fine," Slade replied. "I haven't been on the water for quite a while."

"You've sailed, Mr. Slade?" Gay asked.

"Some," the Ranger admitted, and did not elaborate further.

Only a few hours had passed since Slade had eaten, but with the appetite of lusty youth he was able to put away a second meal without much difficulty. Old Clark, however, outdid his finest efforts with ease. He winked at Gay, who had already finished, hauled out a black pipe and proceeded to stuff it with blacker tobacco. Slade rolled a cigarette.

"Soon as we finish our smoke, we'll mosey," Kendal said, after his old baseburner was drawing satisfactorily. "I've got quite a few business matters to attend to this afternoon — round-up time coming along, you know, so you and Gay can go alone. I'll be here when you get back. All set? Let's go!"

The new boat proved to be a trim little pleasure craft newly painted and furbished. She was cat rigged, her single mast placed far forward, her single sail extended by a long boom. A rather large sail for her size, Slade thought, and would need considerable reefing in a brisk blow. Her small cabin was snug and provided with two bunks, and there was a tiny galley.

"All loaded with chuck in case you get hungry," Kendal said. "All right, the tide's running out. I'll cast off and you can get going. You can circle Mustang Island and give her a good workout in the Gulf. Let's go!"

Kendal cast off. Slade hauled in the line. "You take the tiller and I'll handle the sail," he told his companion. "Okay?"

She nodded. The little boat came about, skimming like a swallow, and began a zig-zag course, almost in the teeth of the wind, toward the point of the island. The girl watched his deft manipulation of the sail.

"I think you must have had considerable experience with sailboats, for — a cowhand, Mr. Slade," she observed.

"I've done a few things other than follow a cow's tail," he replied. He did not think it necessary to elaborate and explain that he had done quite a bit of small boat sailing during his college days.

"By the way," he added, "don't you think we can dispense with the formalities? I grow weary of being 'Mistered' all the time; makes me feel like a first mate on a windjammer."

She shot him a glance through her lashes, then dimpled. "All right — Walt," she said.

"That's better — Gay," he replied. He glanced up at the billowing sail.

"She ought to go along spanking, with this west by south wind, once we get into the Gulf," he remarked. "Handles beautifully, don't you think?"

"A lot better than the one we lost," she answered. "I think Dad has had his eyes on this one for some time. I've a notion he rather welcomed the loss of the other one — gave him an excuse for buying this one. Sometimes I think he missed his calling; he should have been a sailor."

"And you a sailor's wife?"

Again the glance through her lashes. "Would depend on who was the sailor," she replied.

Without mishap they rounded the point and were in the open Gulf. Here, with the wind almost dead astern, the little boat fairly flew, burying her nose in the combers, her foredeck awash. The spray sparkled out from her bow in a myriad of fiery gems. Her wake was a tossing froth of white and gold edged by translucent blue. Slade lashed the boom and stood well forward with one hand on the mast, a striking figure against the background of sky and sea. The girl bent her slender form to the tiller, swaying easily with the heave of the deck. There was color in her creamily tanned cheeks. Her red lips were wet with the flying spray that glinted the sunlight on the unruly hair tossing about her little heart-shaped face. "A Viking and his woman daring an unknown sea" might well have been the title of a great artist's painting had one been there to immortalize them on canvas.

They had covered several miles and were well out in the Gulf, away from the island, when a battered old tramp steamer rounded the distant point behind and plowed along in their wake. Black smoke poured from her squat funnel and she seemed to quiver to the pound of her engines. Slade eyed her with interest as she swiftly overhauled the sailboat.

"Under forced draft," he remarked. "What's got her blasting along like that? You'd think there was a gunboat after her."

The steamer continued to plow along. Now Slade could make out figures leaning on the rail, gazing intently in their direction. They seemed to wear an air of anticipation. His black brows drew together slightly as the tramp closed the distance, holding steadily to her course in the sailboat's wake. Abruptly he turned to Gay.

"Two points west by north," he said.

She glanced at him with puzzled eyes, but obeyed. The boat lurched, buried her bow rail, and veered toward the distant island.

Instantly the steamer changed course and followed in their wake. Slade eyed her with a darkening face.

"Resume course," he told Gay. She did so, and dead in their wake came the steamer, and now she was close, so close they could hear the roar of her funnel and the pound of her racing engines.

"Thought so!" Slade muttered. "Gay," he said, "I'll take the tiller now. You take the sail. Unlash the boom and do just exactly as I tell you, when I tell you. Don't let the boom get away from you and swing around; brace yourself and hang on."

She obeyed without question, her eyes wide, but her hands steady.

"What is that crazy ship trying to do?" she asked, gazing at the approaching steamer.

"In my opinion, she's trying to run us down, and if we don't work lively, that's just what she'll do," Slade replied grimly. "I don't know what this is all about, but that's her intention. Steady now, and do just as I tell you, fast. Get ready to spill the wind out of the sail when I give the word, not before."

Gripping the tiller, he watched the steamer thunder down on them. Now she was less than two hundred yards distant. The figures lining the rail stood tense and staring.

"Spill it!" Slade shouted.

Around swung the boom; the wind spilled out of the sail. The boat lurched, wallowed, came about, burying her gunwale. She righted and shot toward the island, almost at right angles to her former course. Yells and curses rose from the steamer, sounding above the roar of her funnel.

Slade shouted again, "Quick, lash the boom! Take the tiller!"

With swift efficiency, the girl obeyed. Now the steamer was roaring past, her engines working in reverse, striving to turn; she was less than thirty yards distant.

"Try and hold her steady," Slade said, balancing himself on widespread feet. He jerked his right-hand gun and fired at the wheel house, raking the muzzle of the big Colt back and forth.

Suddenly the steamer's bow bobbed and jerked crazily. She wallowed in the trough, righted almost instantly as another man sprang to the wheel. Slade let go with his other gun.

Again the crazy bobbing of the steamer's bow. She rolled and wallowed. And this time she kept on rolling and wallowing until she was out of range of those deadly guns. Slade slammed his Colts back into their holsters and seized the tiller.

"Take the sail," he told Gay; "get it around. We're heading for the island. I see a little cove almost dead ahead. We'll beach her if we have to. They can't follow us there — too shallow. Here we go."

"She's stopped, she's dropping anchor!" Gay exclaimed. Slade nodded, his gaze fixed on the cove, toward which the boat was skimming with increasing speed. A moment later he called,

"Drop the sail and hang onto the mast; we're going to strike."

They did strike seconds later, hard. Gay lost her grip on the mast and was hurled to the deck, but was on her feet again before Slade could reach her. She laughed aloud as his long arm encircled her trim waist.

"This is wonderful!" she shrilled. "Just like pirate days of old."

"Yes, but the pirates didn't have high-power rifles," Slade replied as a slug whined overhead and another struck splinters from the deck. He lifted her in his arms and jumped the railing, landing on the hard packed sand. He lurched, stumbled, caught his balance and scudded for a low sand dune only a few yards distant. Bullets whined past, kicked up spurts of sand at his feet; but he whisked around the end of the dune untouched and flung himself to the ground.

"Made it!" he chuckled breathlessly. "All right, now; they can't shoot through ten feet of sand."

Gay's eyes were blazing. "The dirty murderers!" she stormed. "I hope you killed some of them!"

"Could be," he replied cheerfully. "Anyhow I nicked a couple hard enough to cause them to drop the wheel, and nobody else 'peared anxious to take over the chore until they were out of gun range. Now what are they up to, I wonder? Keep down while I have a look."

Cautiously he raised himself until he could peer over the top of the dune, which was no more than five feet high.

"Be careful! Please be careful!" Gay begged.

"They can't see me against the background of the sand," he answered. He took one quick look and dropped back beside her.

"They're lowering a boat," he said.

"And now what are we going to do?"

"Don't worry, now things will be different," he promised grimly. "Keep down and listen for the oarlocks. Looks to be like somebody out there is plumb loco. Imagine, though, they figured we kept on going behind this ridge, which runs for a couple of miles. They'll get a surprise."

They lay listening until the beat of the oarlocks sounded above the rumble of the surf. Slade waited a few minutes longer, gauging the boat's distance by the sound, when he leaped to his feet.

The boat was within twenty yards of the shore. Five men bent their backs to the oars. Two more stood in the stern, rifles in hand.

Both Slade's guns let go with a rattling crash. One of the rowers slumped forward on his face. Another reeled and fell back. One of the riflemen lurched sideways, fell into the water and sank, leaving a trail of blood on the surface. The remaining oarsmen beat the water to foam as they frantically turned the boat and headed back to the ship, Slade speeding them on their way with a stream of lead hissing over their heads. He watched the boat hoisted to the deck, the anchor hauled up. Smoke boiled from the steamer's funnel as she swung about and roared south by west, for all the world, he thought, like an angry and defeated elephant leaving a lost field.

Gay stood beside him and they watched the vessel until she grew small in the distance and finally vanished in the mists.

"Well, guess that takes care of that," he remarked, reloading and holstering his guns.

"Walt?" she asked, "what was it all about?"

"'Pears somebody doesn't like us," Slade replied.

Her eyes were grave as she regarded him. "I think," she said slowly, "that it was you they were after. I was just an incidental, in the way."

"If so, they were willing to risk murdering you to accomplish their ends," he answered. "Not often you run into an outfit, in this section, that will take chances on killing a woman."

"Well, they didn't do it, and that's what counts," she said gaily. "I suppose you'll think I'm awful, but really I enjoyed the whole episode — it was thrilling."

"I think you're wonderful," he replied impulsively, and meant it. "A girl to ride the river with."

The highest compliment the rangeland can pay.

"Well, you rode the Gulf with me, and it was quite a ride," she said, with a little trill of laughter. "And now I suppose it's prosaic and down to earth after such adventures, but darn it! I'm hungry!"

"Fine!" he applauded. "So am I. And we're stuck here till the tide runs in and floats the boat. I see lots of driftwood about. Suppose we cook here on the beach rather than in that stuffy galley?"

"That will be wonderful," she said. "And it'll be beautiful, sailing back in the moonlight."

"Your father won't worry?"

"Oh, he knows I'm in good hands," she reassured him. "He has great confidence in your — ability."

"Hope he won't be — disillusioned," Slade chuckled, his eyes dancing.

Gay blushed, and did not answer.

Abruptly he turned to face her. "Gay," he said, "will you do something if I ask it?"

Her eyes met his and she looked expectant. "Yes," she answered. "Wh-what is it?"

"You'll be doing me a big favor if you don't mention what happened today — to anybody."

"Is that all!" she said. "Of course I'll do as you say. I don't know why you ask it, but I'll do just as you say."

"Always?" he asked, with laughter in his eyes.

"Always!"

Slade secured provisions and utensils from the galley and built a fire on the beach.

"I'll do the cooking," Gay said. "That's woman's work. Oh, don't worry, I know how. Dad says that any woman, no matter what her economic status, should learn to cook and take care of a house; so I learned. In fact, I like housework and I'm only glad that I'm not forced to go out to make a living, which would force me to be away from it. Otherwise, I wouldn't care; honest work never hurt anybody and is good for one."

The sun had set in flaming splendor before their dinner was ready and the sky was a kaleidescopic marvel of color. The Gulf was bronze and molten gold and the wind had died to a breath.

They ate their dinner by the light of the fire. With the elasticity of youth they had thrown off the cares and anxieties of the day and laughed and joked. After cleaning up they sat silent while the fire died to a glow and the arms of the dark drew near like a loving embrace.

The last spark winked out. The stars veiled their eyes with a bridal veil of fleecy cloud. The little wavelets ran up the beach, advancing, retreating, rising and falling, and only low whispers and soft murmurings broke the scented stillness.

CHAPTER
SEVEN

Some time later, Slade said, "Well, the tide's in, the boat's afloat, and the moon's rising."

"Yes, I suppose we'll have to go," Gay replied, with a sigh. "I hate to leave, it is so lovely here, and everything's been so wonderful."

"Everything?"

"Yes, everything. Do you need to ask?"

Slade carried her to the boat and dropped her lightly on the deck. Then he retrieved the utensils and stowed them away. The wind had shifted and was favorable for the return trip. They sailed the path of the moonbeams, with faith in the future ahead and unforgettable memories behind, and reached Corpus Christi without mishap.

The two-tiered town lay drenched in moonlight and lovely as inspired dream. All about was peace and beauty, or so it seemed.

"This whole south-Texas coast is a veritable Garden of Eden," Slade said. "It has everything that Eden must have had, including — the snakes!"

Kendal was waiting for them in the lobby of the Kinney House.

"Well!" he exclaimed. "Have a nice time?"

"Wonderful!" Gay replied. "We cooked and ate on the beach."

"Fine!" said Kendal. "That is, fine for young folks; old bones hanker for a mite more comfort. Let's go eat."

"At this rate I'll get too fat to be rescued from a burning ship, but, darn it! I am hungry again," Gay agreed.

"Me, too," said Slade, smiling. "Had a lot of exercise today."

"Gosh, chick, but you got a pretty color in your cheeks today," exclaimed old Clark, gazing at his daughter with admiration. "The salt air is good for you."

"Let's eat," said Gay.

They did. Then everybody agreed it was time for bed.

"By the way," said Kendal as they mounted the stairs, "going to sign up with me?"

"Perhaps later," Slade replied. "Tomorrow I'm going to work for Cock Badding down on the waterfront. Will be a change and I've a notion I'll find it interesting. So I'll give it a whirl for a while."

Gay looked disappointed. Kendal shot him a curious look. "Yes, I expect you will find it interesting," he said. "My offer stands."

"I'll be riding out to your place frequently," Slade said. "I gather it's less than ten miles."

"That's right," nodded Kendal. "Not more'n eight. You can't miss it. Big white *casa* set back from the trail about a quarter of a mile. We'll be looking for you; make it soon."

"I will," Slade promised. "In the next day or two."

Slade slept dreamlessly, and if Miss Kendal dreamed, she didn't mention what about.

After breakfast, Slade repaired to the waterfront and found Cock Badding already in his office. The labor contractor greeted him cordially, shot a curious glance at his guns.

"Going to wear 'em on the job?" he asked.

"I'd feel undressed without them," Slade replied.

"Yep, guess you would," Badding nodded. "I think it's a good notion to wear 'em. Sort of rough here at times, and you never can tell, something else might bust loose — like the other night. Sometimes what 'pears to be just a ruckus is used as a cover-up for something bad. Reckon that's been your experience, eh?"

It was Slade's turn to nod. Badding drew a sheaf of papers from a drawer, moved several books closer on the desk, and rose to his feet.

"Okay," he said, "when you get this tangle straightened out, come out on the piers and give me a hand at selecting men for special chores. I've a notion your judgment will be a help. First, now, I'll give you a line-up on things and then you can take over. I've got to hit the piers."

It did not take Slade long to conclude that the "tangle" was not as bad as Cock Badding intimated. He worked steadily for several hours, encountering no real

64

difficulties. Pausing for a smoke now and then, he was straightening out a final invoice when a tall broad-shouldered man entered. He recognized Rance Donner, the ship owner Hayes Wilfred did not like.

Donner did not look particularly "likeable" at the moment. He was plainly irritated and in a thoroughly bad temper.

"Badding around?" he asked abruptly.

"Not just at present," Slade replied. "Is there anything I can do for you? I'm in charge here during his absence."

"My name's Donner, and I want men, a good crew for some special loading, and I want them tonight," the ship owner said, scowling.

"Very well, Mr. Donner, we'll do the very best we can for you," Slade promised.

"Listen!" Donner snapped. "I don't want any of that 'best we can' stuff. I want men, not talk. Do you understand?"

Slade stood up. Tall as he was, Donner had to lift his eyes a trifle to meet El Halcon's steady gray gaze.

"Mr. Donner," he replied, "I said we would do the very best we can for you, and that's just what we'll do. I hope you can understand *that*. Now get out, I'm busy!"

The last words struck Donner with the impact of bullets. He stared, his jaw dropping slightly, started to speak. But something in the cold eyes boring into his seemed to close his lips. He half turned, hesitated. Then abruptly he grinned, a very pleasant grin, Slade thought.

"Mr. Slade — you see I know your name. I guess everybody down here knows it after what you did the other day. Mr. Slade, I'm sorry. I spoke out of turn. I apologize, and I hope you'll see fit to accept my apology in the spirit in which it is given."

"Be glad to, Mr. Donner," Slade replied smilingly. He gestured to a chair. "Suppose you take a load off your feet and have a smoke," he suggested. "I've a notion you could stand a mite of relaxation right now."

Again Donner's eyes widened a little, but he dropped into the chair and accepted the cigarette Slade rolled for him. He spoke after a couple of deep drags.

"That helps," he said. "Yes, I spoke out of turn, but I've been so harrassed by problems and anxieties of late that I'm sort of beside myself, I reckon."

Slade regarded him in silence for several minutes, then,

"Are you ill, Mr. Donner, some disease that's got you worried?" he asked casually. Donner stared.

"If I was any healthier, I reckon I couldn't stand it," he replied.

"Some member of your family ill, in bad shape, got you half sick with foreboding?"

Donner stared again, and looked slightly dazed, hesitated, appeared to turn something over in his mind; he shook his head.

"Got no family," he replied.

"Then it's possible property loss that's got you bothered?"

"Why — why I guess so," Donner answered.

"Weren't you doing all right before you acquired the property?" Slade persisted.

"Guess I was," Donner acceded.

"And don't you think you'd still do all right if you lost the property?"

Rance Donner gazed into the steady eyes that abruptly were warm and understanding. He squared his shoulders, grinned again.

"I get it," he said. "Guess I am an ungrateful cuss. Strong! Well! Not too old! Mr. Slade, you've taught me a mite of a lesson today. One I won't forget. Say! do you take everybody in tow?"

Slade smiled and did not comment. "You'll get your men, Mr. Donner," he said, "even if Cock Badding and I have to lend a hand to fill out."

"And I'll bet the pair of you would get more work done than any six dock wallopers you'll be able to round up," Donner declared with conviction. He stood up, extended his hand, almost diffidently. His clasp was firm and warm; and he left the office whistling.

Slade finished his work and hunted up Cock Badding. "Everything shipshape," he told the contractor.

"Fine!" applauded Badding. "Anybody call while I was out?"

"A gentleman named Rance Donner," Slade replied.

"Donner! He's a cantankerous hellion at times, and salty as they come. How'd you make out with him?"

"Okay," Slade answered. "A little difference of opinion at first, but then he became more reasonable and we had a nice chat. I promised him a crew tonight for a special loading he appears to be worrying about; he was very grateful."

Cock Badding shook his head. "I don't know how you do it," he marvelled. "That rapscallion usually takes the attitude that whatever he wants is coming to him and don't make no bones of saying so. First time I ever heard of him being grateful for something. He's a good account, though, and I'd hate to lose him. Cash on the barrel head, and he pays better than the scale for overtime like tonight. Oswell, the contractor at the other end of the piers, would like to have him. Tried to get him away from me, in fact, for which I didn't thank him. I've a notion that the reason he sticks with me is because I never kowtowed to him much."

"I think you're right," Slade acceded. "He strikes me as the sort to respect a man who isn't afraid to talk up to him."

"Then I've a notion he did a lot of 'respecting' today," Badding grinned. "There's some funny yarns going around about him, but I don't pay 'em no mind. Figure they're none of my business. So long as he plays square with me."

"The right idea," Slade agreed. "Snap judgment in such matters is not good. Liable to do somebody an injustice."

"That's the way I figure it," nodded Badding.

"So I gathered the other night," Slade smiled.

"Huh! to heck with what anybody says about *you!*" growled Badding. "You're the bully boy with a glass eye for my money, and I don't give a hang who knows it. Let's go get something to eat — it's past noon. Then we'll round up a crew for Donner. I think I'll stick around for a while tonight and see to it that everything goes as it should go."

"I'll stay with you," Slade said.

"Fine!" exclaimed Badding. "Be plumb glad to have your company. Here's a good place to eat."

While they were awaiting their orders, Slade remarked:

"Yesterday when Miss Kendal and I were sailing, a battered old steamer passed us, and she sure was high-tailing. Name wasn't legible from a distance. I was wondering if you noticed her; she put out from here."

"Yep, I noticed her," Badding replied. "Went with the tide not long after noon. That was the Iago di Compostella, Spanish registry. A regular tropic tramp if there ever was one. Crew looks like what a nest of pirates are supposed to look like. Captain a hangdog hellion with a knife scar splitting his face in two and a cast in one eye. I remember her because we loaded her and because all of a sudden she was in one heck of a hurry to get under way. We'd been loading regular and she had almost her full cargo when down came the captain and begged us to finish up fast. Handed the boys a fistful of pesos to sift sand with the last few loads. You'd have thought he had a date with a *senorita* and was scairt the other feller would get ahead of him. She went out under forced draft, just a-boomin'."

"Has she docked here before?" Slade asked idly.

"Uh-huh," replied Badding, preparing to tackle his chuck. "Been here several times. The sort you wouldn't want to meet down a dark alley at night, but her papers are always in order and her crew behaves in port. Drink together in the saloons and don't mix much. She loads hides and tallow and also packs charcoal, sulphur and saltpeter. I noticed 'em on her manifest."

"Charcoal, sulphur and saltpeter, or potassium nitrate," Slade repeated. "Funny mixture."

"Uh-huh, ain't it?" nodded Badding, "but it's part of what she packs. Let's eat!"

Slade asked no more questions, but he considered what he had learned quite interesting. Charcoal, sulphur, and potassium nitrate! Mix 'em in the proper proportions and you have gunpowder!

CHAPTER
EIGHT

Conversation ceased. Badding was absorbed in his food, Slade busy with his thoughts. He had not by any manner of means made up his mind concerning Rance Donner. The ship owner had a pleasing personality when he wished to employ it, but he was also an individual of uncertain temper. Also, Slade judged, he was intensely ambitious and anxious to get ahead in the world. And ambition all too often begets ruthlessness and scant regard for the rights and the well being of others. There was more than a hint that Donner would brush aside opposition with an intolerant hand, and if necessary that hand would be heavy; and Donner would quite probably justify, to himself, the means by what results they produced. All too often the only law such men respected was the law of the jungle — the survival of the fittest — with their own peculiar and casuistic definition of the fittest as their guiding star. Rance Donner might well fall into that category. On the other hand, he might be maligned, the victim of jealousy and envy, or of mere idle gossip. Both angles must be considered, weighed and resolved into their proper perspective. His judgment must be held in abeyance until he learned more concerning Rance Donner and evaluated what he learned.

There was no doubt but that serious trouble of some sort had already built up on the Corpus Christi waterfront, instigated by somebody who held human life lightly, to put it mildly. Wanton murder had been committed, other murders attempted. Somebody had suborned or bribed the callous skipper of the tropic tramp into getting rid of himself, evidently considered a menace and in somebody's way. He rather doubted that the steamer captain was a member of the outfit, whatever and whoever it was. Quite likely he had merely been paid to do a chore and no questions asked. However, it must be considered that he could be a member of the organization; his peculiar cargo was something that required a mite of explaining. And after the blowing up of the windjammer Albatross, anything having to do with explosives was not to be altogether ignored.

He wondered if the tramp would put in at Corpus Christi again, and thought that very probably she would. It was logical to assume the skipper would reason that El Halcon the outlaw would hardly report the outrage to the authorities and quite likely persuade the girl not to. Which would leave him with only possible corporal reprisals to contend with, and that doubtless would not deter such a hardbitten hellion as he evidently was. Slade chuckled to himself as he admitted that if the skipper's train of thought did follow such channels he was plotting a true course. He, Slade, did *not* report the incident to the authorities and he did

72

persuade Gay Kendal not to do so. He hoped he had sized up the situation correctly, for he would be pleased if the Iago di Compostella did drop anchor in Corpus Christi harbor again. Such men as Badding described the skipper as being, while arrogant bullies when things were going their way, usually were not noted for courage when the tide turned against them. Slade felt that quite likely the skipper of the tramp would hang his grandmother to save his own skin and would very likely talk under a little gentle persuasion.

Cock Badding pushed back his empty plate and began manufacturing a cigarette.

"We'll have a smoke," he said, "and then if it's okay with you we'll go round up a crew for Rance Donner. I'd like to have your judgment on the jiggers; I've a notion it's dependable."

Badding looked somewhat askance at the first man Slade picked from a group eating lunch. He was a brawny individual with carroty red hair, and underslung jaw, greenish eyes, and a face puckered with the scars of old wounds.

"Be glad to take it on," the man replied when Slade broached the subject of overtime that night. "I can use the money. Name's Norton, Chuck Norton."

Slade recruited half a dozen more from the first group and then passed on to another bunch.

"That feller Norton," Badding observed dubiously. "Sort of an unsavory galoot, don't you think?"

"Got a good nose," Slade replied.

"A good *nose!*" Badding repeated. "What the devil?"

"It's a nice straight nose, and the tip turns up like a child's," Slade explained composedly. "I figure a jigger with a nose like that is dependable."

Cock Badding laughed heartily. "I never thought of it, but somehow it makes sense," he admitted. "All of a sudden that jigger does look sort of different."

It did not take long to enlist a crew of a score and more for the night work, and Badding let Slade pick them all.

"Now I'm heading for the other end of the dock," he announced. "You stick around the office while I'm gone and take care of anything that shows up."

When Badding returned to the office, some hours later, he gave Slade a peculiar look.

"That feller Norton," he said. "I was sorta curious and questioned some of the boys about him. They told me he sends all his overtime money, and he works plenty of it, to an old mother in Galveston, and that he got that bad scar on his left cheek from diving into breakers during a storm to keep a jigger who'd fell overboard from drowning."

"Well?" Slade smiled.

"Well," said Badding, "from now on I'm going to pay attention to noses."

At about the same time a discussion was under way between Chuck Norton and some of his mates.

"The notorious El Halcon, the outlaw, eh?" remarked Norton.

"What do you think of him, Chuck?" somebody asked.

74

"What do I think of him! I think he's a man I'd like to have beside me during a China Sea typhoon with the main gone, a jury midden, the decks awash, and the forepeak raffle to clear in a hundred-mile wind with your claspknife in your teeth! That's what I think of him. What a bucko mate he'd make! I'd sure like the chance to sail under him." The others nodded grave agreement.

Chuck Norton was to get his wish, unpleasantly.

In the office, Badding glanced at his watch. "Nearly five, time to knock off," he announced. "Donner won't want his crew till eight."

"Then I think I'll pay my horse a visit and go to the hotel to freshen up a bit," Slade said. "I'll meet you here a little before eight. Okay?"

"Okay," Badding nodded. "Say, you sure made a hit with Donner. He couldn't stop talking about you. Said you gave him a slant on things he'd never thought of before and that it did him a lot of good. You hogtied the account with him, and I appreciate it. Feller, you sure have a way with folks. How do you do it?"

"Mostly by letting them do most of the talking," Slade smiled.

"Guess you got something there," Badding conceded. "Good listeners ain't easy to come by. Well, so long; see you at eight."

Slade found Shadow in a fairly good temper but restless.

"I know," Slade told him. "You don't like to be cooped up this way. I'll give you a chance to stretch your legs soon. We'll amble over and see old Clark Kendal. So take it easy and don't snort your teeth loose. Be seeing you."

After a shave and a bath and something to eat, Slade felt much refreshed. He smoked a cigarette in the hotel lobby and then sauntered to the bar to look things over. Standing nearby was Hayes Wilfred, the grotesque dwarf ship owner.

Wilfred greeted him cordially and insisted he have a drink.

"Understand you're working for Badding," he remarked. "A good man, from all I've heard of him. Personally I've had only a superficial contact with him. Oswell handles my loading crews."

Oswell, Slade recalled, was the labor contractor at the other end of the piers who had tried to get the Donner account away from Cock Badding.

"I fancy you will profit from signing up with Badding," Wilfred observed. "But isn't it a somewhat unusual choice of occupation for a — cowhand?"

"Perhaps, for a — cowhand," Slade smiled.

Wilfred flushed a little. "I didn't intend my remark as disparaging to cowhands," he said, "but I've noticed that a cowboy usually stays with ranch work."

"Perhaps it is because ranch work is all the majority of them know," Slade replied. "A cowhand is in something the same category as a sailor, whose life is also not an easy one. The cowhand has security; the ranch is home, just as the ship is the sailor's home. And he seldom has to consider the hazard of unemployment; a ranch owner hangs onto his hands, if humanly possible, in bad times as well as good."

"I can understand that," Wilfred nodded. "But security is the deadly foe of ambition."

"Yes," Slade replied, "But if I may venture to paraphrase your remark, ambition is all too often the deadly foe of content."

"Possibly," Wilfred conceded, "but, Mr. Slade, what is content?"

"Content," Slade answered slowly, "is the soothing shadow of God's hand."

Wilfred gazed at him a moment in silence, then, "Your mode of expression, Mr. Slade, is also unusual for —" He hesitated.

"For a cowhand," Slade completed, still smiling.

Wilfred laughed. "We appear to have drifted into a somewhat *unusual* discussion, to again employ the word we've been working overtime," he said.

"Which reminds me, I'll have to be going," Slade replied. "We have some overtime loading tonight, for Rance Donner."

Wilfred's eyes narrowed a trifle. "A man who is *not* devoid of ambition," he commented.

"But who perhaps is somewhat lacking in content," Slade countered. "Well, I really must be going. It's been a pleasure to talk with you, Mr. Wilfred."

"The conclusion is mutual, then," Wilfred returned, with a smile. "Good night, Mr. Slade."

Arriving at the office shortly before eight, Slade found the crew already assembled, cracking jokes and indulging in jovial profanity directed at one another, including questionable ancestry, not commendable present, and dubious future. Cock Badding was sitting with his feet propped on the desk, smoking a cigar.

"Just waiting for Donner," he said. "The wagons were already pulling onto the pier when I came past. A lot of big fellows and loaded to capacity. Will take till midnight to stow all that stuff."

"The more time, the more money," Chuck Norton observed cheerfully. "We can use it, eh, boys?" There was a general nodding of heads.

Rance Donner showed up a few minutes later. He greeted Slade with a smile and a nod.

"All set to go?" he asked. "Fine! The old Glengarry's waiting to be fed. I hope to sail with the tide."

"You'll make it," Slade promised. "Got a fine crew for you, that is if they don't pack the ship off and trade her for redeye."

"I wouldn't put it past 'em," chuckled Donner, running his eye over the hardbitten assemblage. "A pocketful of pesos will be easier to pack though."

A general laugh greeted the sally and the crew trooped out with Slade in the lead.

The Glengarry proved to be a battered old brigantine in need of paint, but Slade thought her hull appeared sound, her two masts and other spars in good shape, her cordage and her sails new. She was square-rigged, but unlike a brig, she did not carry a square mainsail. She looked as if she had speed.

The ponderous freighting wagons were lined up on the pier, loaded with tightly nailed packing cases, some square, others rectangular, and they were heavy. Slade

78

wondered what the devil they contained but preferred not to ask Donner.

Donner himself looked complacent as he watched the crew at work.

"Best bunch I ever saw," he declared. "Mr. Slade, you sure know how to pick 'em. We'll make the tide easy, the way those dock wallopers handle the stuff."

"Yes, we'll make it, barring unforeseen complications," Slade agreed.

The "complications" were due to commence without delay. Chuck Norton and a couple of his chosen mates were down in the upper after-hold, helping the sailors trim cargo, and spewing profanity through the hatch, with sarcastic comments anent paper-back snails who couldn't lift a pound of feathers.

It was Norton who discovered the fire; but a moment before, Slade had heard the muffled explosion in the bowels of the vessel. It wasn't loud, more like a sharp thud, as if some heavy object had been dropped, but he instantly knew something was wrong. He was going down the ladder hand over hand when Norton's bull-bellow shook the timbers —

"Smoke bilin' up from the lower hold!"

Slade took in the situation at a glance. "Water!" he thundered. "Form a bucket brigade! Get pans, boilers from the galley! Anything that will hold water! Move!"

A moment later he was in the lower hold, Norton beside him. A huge heap of oil-soaked waste and other inflammables was burning fiercely, the flames already hungrily licking the timbers, which were beginning to smolder.

Down came the water, borne by cursing, wildly excited men. Slade and Norton sloshed it on the fire. Already the heat was terrific, the hold thick with smoke.

At first they seemed to make no headway against the flames, which defied the constant drowning.

"Maybe!" muttered Norton. "Maybe!"

"We'll do it," Slade said, edging closer to the fire and emptying the contents of a huge boiler. "Hightail with that water!" he shouted.

Suddenly Rance Donner's voice came ringing down the hatch —

"Slade! Norton! get out of there. Off this infernal ship. Let her burn. Come out, I say!"

"You go to hell!" Norton bawled back. "We got a fire to put out! Water!"

The smoke thickened as the deluge of water gained the ascendancy. Both men were choking and coughing. Slade experienced a queer feeling of lightness. His hands fumbled, his eyes snarted. But still he sloshed water over the flickers, moving closer to drench the smoldering timbers.

"I think that does it," he said thickly.

There was no answer from his companion. Turning, he saw, by the dim lantern light filtering into the hold, Chuck Norton prone on the floor, as out as the fire.

CHAPTER
NINE

Muttering, Slade picked up his heavy form and staggered to where men with unneeded water were descending.

"Lend a hand," he said hoarsely. "Get him to the outer air before he takes the Big Jump! Move!"

Ready hands grasped the unconscious longshoreman. A chain of men hove him upward and laid him on the deck. Slade followed, slowly, for he was unutterably weary and far from in good shape himself. The first man he contacted upon reaching the deck and the blessed fresh air was Rance Donner. The ship owner's eyes were wild, his face strained.

"That was touch and go," he said. "If those packing cases had really got going good, we'd have all been blown to Mexico!"

"What's in them?" Slade asked.

"Celluloid sheets and strips," Donner replied. Slade whistled under his breath.

"You're right," he said. "That stuff is so inflammable that in large quantities it burns with explosive violence and generates a gas as bad as gunpowder. Okay, though, we got the fire out without too much trouble and all set to keep on loading. You'll make the tide."

81

"Yes," Donner said dully. "Yes, I reckon we will. The stuff is consigned to a firm in Bluefields, Nicaragua. They make it into Christmas toys. Late in the year already and they are behind in their orders. That's why I am so anxious to get it going tonight. But I didn't want you to take such a chance. After all, the blasted ship is only property," he added with a wan smile.

"Yes, but there's no sense in allowing property to be destroyed if it's possible to prevent it." Slade answered. "Don't take my little homily of this afternoon *too* literally, Mr. Donner."

"Yes, but when a valuable life is at stake, to the devil with property," replied Donner.

Slade called his men together. "As soon as the smoke clears a little, I want that hold combed from end to end to make sure there's nothing else off-color lying around," he told them.

Norton had been revived and was on his feet expressing his profane opinion of everything in general. He turned to Slade.

"Figure that fire was set?" he asked in low tones.

"Definitely," Slade answered. "Some sort of clockwork mechanism, I'd say. Set to explode a small fire bomb of one kind or another. I've a notion," he added thoughtfully, "that somebody slipped a mite when he set the contraption. I'd say it was intended to go off after the ship was out at sea, but the timing mechanism was off a bit."

Norton swore viciously. "The blankety-blank-blank murdering skunks!" he concluded. "I know what it is to be in a fire at sea. You end up in a cockleshell a hundred miles from shore and all you need is a stiff Gulf blow to send you to Davy Jones' locker. What in blazes is this waterfront coming to, anyhow?"

"I'd say it's fast becoming the Devil's branding pen," observed Cock Badding, who had overheard the conversation. "Who in Halifax is at the bottom of it all, I wonder? The whole business doesn't seem to make sense, but somebody must stand to profit by it, in one way or another. Such things aren't done without a reason. What do you think, Slade?"

"Learn the reason and you'll very likely learn who's pulling the strings," the Ranger replied.

His hearers nodded.

The hold was searched and nothing sinister was discovered. The loading was resumed and completed without further incident. Cock Badding heaved a sigh of relief as the last case was safely carried aboard and stowed.

"There you are," he told Donner. "You can sail with the tide."

"Right!" agreed the ship owner. He drew forth a wad of money. "Here's the pay, and a little bonus for saving the blasted ship," he said. The longshoremen raised a cheer.

"It'll all be gone come morning, the chances are, and they'll show up with busted heads and pains in their tempers," chuckled Badding as he began handing out the dinero.

Donner turned to Slade, who smiled. Donner also smiled, put up his money and extended his hand.

"Thank you, for everything," he said.

As they walked back to the office together, Badding remarked, "Well, everything went off satisfactorily, despite complications, and we've sure got the Donner account solid, thanks largely to you."

Slade nodded, but personally he was not at all satisfied with everything. In the first place, he was convinced that Rance Donner knew more about the attempt to burn his ship than he chose to divulge. Slade had a hunch that not unlikely Donner had a very good notion who was back of the attempt but for reasons of his own preferred not to mention any names. Just what those reasons were, Slade had no definite idea. But sometimes men are not in a position to level charges against others. A judicial axiom is that if you go to court, you'd better go in with clean hands. That could be the case with Donner.

Secondly, he had only Donner's word that the contents of the packing cases were celluloid sheets and not something more lethal and more hazardous when coming into contact with fire. Of course, the Customs people should have taken care of that, but there was always the chance that somebody had been suborned; bribed not to investigate a shipment too closely. Such things had happened. He was inclined to believe Donner, but was forced to admit that he could be mistaken, and in such matters a Ranger could not afford to be mistaken.

Thoroughly tired out, Slade had a bath and went to bed. He slept soundly and awakened to a day of brilliant sunshine with a crisp touch of Autumn in the air. He arose in plenty of time for a leisurely breakfast, after which he made his way to the office.

Badding was in a cheerful mood and for a while they talked over the stirring happenings of the night before.

"Well, the Glengarry is on her way rejoicing," Badding observed.

"Guess Donner feels pretty good today. Expect he'll drop in some time for a gab. Not a bad jigger when he takes a notion to act nice, and he sure was grateful last night. Losing that ship would have hit him hard, I reckon, and for a while it sure looked like he would lose her. Some hellion made a nice try, all right, and if it hadn't been for you and Norton I've a notion he'd have gotten away with it. Feller, you sure have raised Hades and shoved a chunk under a corner since you coiled your twine here."

"Not of my choosing," Slade replied with a smile.

"Nope, I guess not," Badding conceded. He chuckled. "I was thinking of what Sheriff Cole said the other night," he added. "About trouble busting loose wherever you showed up. Looks like he sort of had the right of it — trouble for some people I figure have some trouble coming. Hello, here comes Donner now."

The ship owner entered with a cordial greeting for both. "Will have another job of loading this afternoon, the Cambria," he said. "Badding, I'd sure take it as a favor if you could supply me with the same gang we had last night. A bit better than the regular scale for those hustlers. Can you arrange it?"

"Why, I guess I can," Badding replied. "Can't we, Walt?"

"I'll go round them up right away," Slade promised. "When do you want them, Mr. Donner?"

"Two o'clock okay?"

"Two o'clock it will be," Slade replied.

"Fine!" said Donner. "See you then; I got to hustle now, a lot to do."

"Well, here's hoping this one will be a mite more peaceful than last night," remarked Badding.

"At least I'm hoping there will be no more fires," Slade said. "I'm sort of fed up with heat and smoke."

"I should imagine you would be," nodded Badding. "Don't count too heavy on it, though; they say things always go in threes."

As Badding predicted, there were some sore heads and sore tempers among the turbulent twenty, but all were cheerful and ready for work. Slade had them set for the Cambria at two o'clock sharp. Donner's promise of extra pay for the chore improved tempers and caused cuts and bruises to be forgotten.

"Only if I keep on hauling in the dinero this way, I'll never get any sleep or be plumb sober again," a husky named Shadwell lamented.

"*Again!*" jeered a six-foot-two Welshman whose name was so unpronounceable that he was known only as Runt. "When were you ever sober?"

"I don't see why Mr. Slade picked either one of you," observed Norton. "To act as horrible examples for the rest of us, I guess."

Slade knew that both were Norton's particular cronies and had the night before shown a capacity for work almost equal to that of big Chuck himself.

The Cambria was another windjammer, a schooner. Like the Glengarry, while pretty well battered, she looked seaworthy enough. Evidently Donner did not skimp on the essentials.

"Good grub on his ships, too," said Norton when Slade commented on her efficient appearance. "Good grub and a tot of grog every morning to open your eyes and sweeten your bilge. He's a first-rate owner. A hard man but a square one."

That, it appeared, was the concensus of opinion relative to Rance Donner; plenty salty when he needed to be, but a man of his word who was just to his employees, asking only a good day's work and willing to pay for it.

All of which was in Donner's favor but still did not clear him of such possible questionable practices as gun running or other contraband activities with their attendant violence and disregard for the law in general.

On the way to the Cambria's loading pier they passed a trim brig just putting out. She gleamed with fresh paint and snowy canvas.

"The Beddington, one of Hayes Wilfred's tubs," Norton volunteered. "He keeps his ships looking like a millionaire's yacht."

"Good man to work for?" Slade asked.

Norton frowned a little. "Cuts rations close and no grog," he replied. "Never pays above the scale like Donner does at times. Says his margin of profit is too small for him to hand out gratuties, as he calls extra pay. Square with his men, but that's all. Cash on the barrel head always. Never asks his boys to wait a little for their pay, as Donner sometimes has to do."

"How do Donner's men take that?" Slade queried.

"They take it as it comes and are always willing to go along with him," Norton answered. "They know just how he stands — he never holds back anything from them — and stand by him in tough times just as he stands by them. He's been known to take on hands who are really in no shape for work, just because they sailed with him before. You'll see a sick man on his decks doing the very best he can and maybe a bit more than he should. A feller has to have something worth while in him to get that sort of thing out of a man."

Slade nodded sober agreement. If Rance Donner really was violating the law in one way or another, bringing him to justice was not going to be a chore the Ranger would enjoy.

CHAPTER
TEN

Donner stuck around while the loading got under way, but did not attempt to advise or interfere; he appeared content to allow Slade to manage affairs.

Meanwhile Slade was studying the ship owner, the concentration furrow deepening between his black brows. Although he was positive that he had never seen Rance Donner prior to the previous day, he experienced a persistent feeling that the man's countenance was familiar. Donner reminded him strongly, in feature and expression, of someone he had seen no long time before. The sort of resemblance called to mind upon meeting the subject of a photograph, a subtle similarity that while vague is nevertheless definite. He wracked his brains for a clue to the explanation, and found none. Donner looked like somebody, but who that somebody might be he hadn't the slightest notion. But he was sure it was not just a "passing on the street" impression. Recently he had met or talked with somebody whom Donner greatly resembled. Oh, the devil with it! Would come to him eventually, of that he was sure. He turned his attention to supervising the activities of his men.

The loading of the Cambria progressed smoothly with no untoward incident. Full dark had fallen, however, before the chore was completed and the men paid off. Badding was busy elsewhere, so Slade collected his fee and stowed it in the office safe. The longshoremen were making ready for a night on the town.

"Matey, why don't you come along with me and Shadwell and Runt?" invited Norton. "Everything's under control and you've earned a bit of fun same as the rest of us. We'll drop in at some lively places. What say?"

"All right," Slade replied. "I think I can stand a mite of diversion. You lead the way and I'll follow your trail. Wait till I lock the office; I've no idea when Badding will be back."

The chore attended to, they crossed the pier and cruised along Water Street.

"First off here's a place we'll drop anchor in," said Norton, pausing before a window lighted with a rosy glow. Over the swinging doors came strains of soft music.

"It's a Mexican place," Norton explained. "Nice sociable swabs, good music, good likker, and purty *senoritas*. I've a notion you'll like it."

They pushed through the swinging doors and filed into a big room that boasted a long bar, a lunch counter, tables for leisurely eaters, gaming tables, a dance floor and a really good Mexican orchestra.

As they entered, heads turned and all eyes were fixed on Walt Slade's tall form.

"El Halcon!" the whisper ran from group to group. "El Halcon! The friend of the lowly!"

Norton twinkled his green eyes at Slade. "Matey, they know you here," he chuckled. "Yep, they sure do; or know of you."

A waiter bowed low and escorted them to a table. The owner, fat, jovial, with alert eyes, came hurrying forward and his bow eclipsed the waiter's.

"*Capitan!*" he exclaimed. "Truly am I honored! Drinks for you and your *amigos? Si*, at once, but you cannot pay. You are my guests, I repeat, I am honored."

Norton chuckled again. "Having you come along, matey, was sure a prime notion," he said. "Looks like they're ready to turn over their whole manifest for us to take our pick from."

Glasses and a bottle were quickly forthcoming, brought by the proprietor himself. He filled the glasses to the brim, and one for himself.

"To our honored guest," he said, raising his glass.

"*Gracias*," Slade replied, rising to his feet, "and to one whom it is an honor to know."

His bow was as courtly and somewhat more graceful than the owner's, whose body wasn't built to bend that way. Norton and the others ducked their heads and grinned. The owner smiled, bowed again, gestured meaningly to the full bottle and hurried off to attend to his multitudinous duties. One of which consisted of a low-voice consultation with the orchestra leader. A few minutes later that worthy also approached the table and bowed profoundly. In his hand he carried a guitar.

"*Capitan*, will not you do us the great favor, *si*? Will not you sing for us as only El Halcon can sing?"

"Sure he will!" boomed big Chuck. "Won't you, Matey? Give us a real deep water chantey." Shadwell and Runt voiced noisy assent.

"Well, I guess it's the only way I can keep you hellions quiet," Slade said.

The orchestra leader led the way to the platform in the manner of a commanding general leading a triumphant march. He handed Slade the guitar, bowed low and held up his hand for silence. Instantly there was an expectant hush and all eyes were fixed on Slade.

He took the guitar, ran his slim fingers over the strings with crisp power and played a soft prelude. Glancing about he saw that there were other seamen present and, mindful of Chuck Norton's request, he sang —

I'm tired of streets and cities
And the endless talk of men,
So I've found a tramp windjammer
And I'm shipping out again.

I'm going where the combers
Break in thunder o'er the rail
While the moonlight spills its silver
On the wind-filled bellying sail.

Oh, life is worth the living
When a Norther thunders down,
And the very ocean trembles
At the heavens' lowering frown!

When with shrieking sky above us
And the raging sea beneath,
We go up to clear the raffle
With our clasp-knives in our teeth.

And there ne'er was time for dreaming
Like the blazing tropic night,
When the racing waves are flame-touched
And the wake's a welt of light.

Oh, I've heard the voices calling
O'er the spreading watery miles,
From the crashing polar ice-floes,
From the little coral isles —

And my heart is singing answer,
So I've left the haunts of men;
And I'm facing toward the morning,
For I'm shipping out again!

As the great golden baritone-bass, deep and sonorous
as the breakers storming on a reef, sweet as the murmur
of the breezes in the palms, pealed and thundered, the
room was hushed. Games were forgotten. Glasses rested
untasted on the bar. The dance floor girls stood wide-
eyed, gazing at the tall singer of dreams.

With a crash of chords the music ceased and Slade
stood smiling at the chorus of "*vivas*" and the clapping
of hands.

"Another, matey, give us another!" boomed Norton.
A score of voices seconded the request.

Slade gave them another, a dreamy love song of *Mejico* which held his audience entranced. With a smile and a bow he returned the guitar to its owner and joined Norton and the others at the table.

"Matey, I sure can't figure why you waste time hanging around a waterfront," Norton said. "You ought to be in grand opry."

"You're prejudiced," Slade replied smilingly.

"The singingest man in the Southwest," remarked Shadwell. "Guess that's plumb right. Blazes! here's the captain of this scow bearing down on us with another bottle! We'll never get out of here!"

As he sipped his drink, while his companions did full justice to theirs, Slade studied the gathering and listened to all his keen ears could overhear. It was not only because he craved a mite of relaxation that he had agreed to join Norton and the others in their cruise of waterfront bars. Drink opens men's lips and some chance remark he might catch could possibly provide a clue to the mystery that was plaguing the piers. Back of it all, Slade felt sure, was a mastermind directing operations and until he could obtain some inkling as to whom that mastermind was, he had little chance of clearing up the mess. Perhaps the night would produce something helpful. He hoped so and was prepared to take advantage of any opportunity that might present.

A little later, after saying goodbye to their affable host, the *cantina* owner, and replying to the multitude of "come agains" called by the gathering, they shoved off for another port, as Norton put it.

They made a number of stops, finally pausing at a rather dingy, dimly lighted place that Slade thought interesting despite some questionable appearing characters at the bar and a bristle-headed drink juggler who looked like something escaped from a piracy melodrama.

But he was growing a bit drowsy and decided this was his last stop for the night. He hoped he would be able to persuade his companions to call it a night also, for their potations had been liberal, to put it mildly.

Again they occupied a table. Drinks were brought by a slovenly waiter. Slade tasted his and concluded that the whiskey here was in keeping with the surroundings. It was inferior to the other drinks he had sampled, having a slightly bitter taste. He threw it down at a gulp to get rid of it, watched his companions down theirs. He was very, very drowsy. Remarkably so, in fact. Yes, this was certainly his last one. Again he glanced at the others. He was vaguely surprised to see that both Norton and Runt had pillowed their heads on their folded arms, and that Shadwell was nodding, his eyes closed.

Norton and Runt had the right notion; they were fast asleep. Time to get out and go to bed; he was so blasted drowsy! He leaned forward a little. Before he realized it, he was emulating the example of the others. His head was pillowed on his arms. Mighty comfortable; he'd rest a minute, then rout out his companions and go to bed. In — just — a minute.

Dimly he sensed that hands were fumbling him. Something wasn't as it should be. He jerked erect. A blaze of white light dazzled his eyes, and a rush of pain flowing through a head and limbs that were not his own. Then blackness.

CHAPTER
ELEVEN

Walt Slade was riding through a thick and gloomy wood. The road was so rough his horse lurched and swayed till he could hardly stay in the saddle. A particularly violent lurch slammed him against one of the nearby trunks. He cursed the road, told Shadow a thing or two, and was rewarded by another stunning bump. It was so dark under the trees he could barely make out the shadowy shapes of the branches arching just above his head.

He strained his eyes to see them better. Gradually they took form. To his astonishment they weren't branches at all, but stout wooden beams supporting rough planking. As he pondered this phenomenon, still another lurch was followed by another violent impact. Slade realized he wasn't banging against tree trunks but a wooden bulkhead. His mind whirled back to something like normal and he glanced about.

He was lying on a dirty bunk in a poorly lighted room. There were other bunks, a dozen or more, built in double tiers against the walls. On three of them lay motionless forms. One head boasted a thatch of bristly red hair. Slade stared in astonishment. The sleeper was undoubtedly Chuck Norton. Gradually he catalogued the other two as Shadwell and Runt. And the lurching was not that of a laboring horse, but the jerk and sway of a vessel on rough water; he was in the forecastle of a ship!

Instinctively both hands dropped to his thighs and he muttered an oath. His guns and his double cartridge belts were gone. But his broad leather waist belt, in the cunningly concealed secret pocket of which was money and the silver star of the Rangers, had not been touched.

Gradually he began realizing other things. His head was one vast ache and there was a lump on the back of it. He ached all over. There was a bitter, feathery taste in his mouth.

With the knowledge came fuller understanding. That last drink in the dingy saloon, the drink with a bitter taste which he had gulped quickly to get rid of the blasted stuff in a hurry. That drink had been drugged! A stiff shot of chlorodyne or something very like it.

A flame of furious anger enveloped him, directed chiefly at himself. A trap had been set for him and he had walked into it like a dumb yearling. Drugged! and shanghaied onto some infernal ship bound for the devil only knew where. Setting his teeth grimly against the pain in his head, he swung his legs over the edge of the bunk and dropped to the floor to stand weaving for a moment. Poor Chuck and the others! They had been taken along, too, perhaps because they were in his company. Now what the devil was to be done!

Overhead he could hear a patter of steps; he turned at a closer sound. A pair of enormous feet were descending the ladder which led upward to the forecastle scuttle. An instant later their owner dropped lightly to the floor.

He was a huge man with thick, bowed shoulders and long, hairy arms. His face was seamed with old scars and he had a broken nose, a square jaw and little eyes set deep in his head.

"So, slept off your jag, eh?" he rumbled. "All right, my man, on deck with you. There's work to do."

Slade's eyes narrowed. "What the devil are you talking about?" he demanded.

The answer was a crashing blow in the face. It hurled him back against the tier of bunks, but it also jolted the last of the cobwebs from his brain, and the big seaman learned he had caught a Tartar. A sizzling left hook laid his cheek open to the bone. A straight right stretched him on his back, bawling for help.

Three more big men came sliding down the ladder. Slade met the first one, whose face was split by a long and jagged scar and who had a cast in one eye, with an uppercut that spurted blood from his lips and sent him to the floor beside the first man, who was scrambling to his feet to join in the attack.

Ducking, weaving, Slade met the four of them with lefts and rights that punished. But the odds were too heavy. He was borne down by sheer weight of numbers and was the recipient of brutal kicks. Chuck Norton, Shadwell and Runt, awakened by the uproar, came scrambling from their bunks, but the scar-faced man, who was the captain of the ship, pulled a gun and held them at bay.

The two mates and the bo'sun, for such they were, shoved and beat and kicked Slade up the ladder to the deck. At gunpoint, the scar-faced captain herded the others after him.

On the deck, the captain, swabbing his bleeding mouth, glared at Slade with maniacal fury. His raucous bellow shook the air —

"All hands aft to witness punishment! Trice him up! Ten lashes! It's mutiny! Lend a hand here!"

Slade was hauled to the main mast. He knew what was in store for him, but he did not fight back. His cool, keen brain was now in the ascendancy and he knew that further resistance would very likely just get him a bullet. Wait!

The first mate, whose name, Slade learned later was Parsons, stripped off his shirt and with the deftness of long practice bound him to the mast. His hands raised high, his body exposed for the lash, but otherwise unrestrained.

The sailors had moved up with a shuffling of feet, muttering among themselves.

"Belay that gab!" shouted the mate. "All right, bo'sun, lay on."

The bo'sun, squat, ungainly, but powerful of build, strode forward, in his hand a short stock of wood from which depended nine lengths of knotty rope — the dreaded "cat-'o-nine-tails." Slade's anger rose again until it almost choked him, but he said nothing, just braced himself against the descending multiple lashes.

It was all he could do to keep from flinching from the nine simultaneous bites of the whip. He rose slightly on his toes despite his effort not to do so.

"One!" counted the mate.

The lashes whistled through the air and cut into the welts the first blow had raised. Slade set his teeth and endured the pain in grim silence.

"Two!" counted the mate.

Again the burning, biting slash of the multiple ropes. And again! And again!

"Five! Five more to go!"

Slade's body was a flame of agony. Sweat burst out on his face. There was a salty taste on his lips. He realized that blood was spurting over his shoulder, splashing back into his face, staining the mast, trickling to the deck.

"Eight!" counted the mate.

The wave of agony coursed from Slade's loins to his shoulders. There was a dull roaring in his ears. The ache of his fettered wrists was just one more incident to the web of torment that enmeshed him. More blood spattered the deck. He set his teeth and held on.

"Ten!" chanted the mate. "Cut him down!"

Slade's wrists were released. He turned slowly to face the captain.

"Ready to go to work now?" the skipper asked in a snarling voice.

"Yes, I'm ready to go to work," Slade replied quietly. He glanced toward where Chuck Norton and the others stood, their faces convulsed with rage, and shook his head the merest trifle. No sense in them getting a taste of the lash, which would do none of them any good.

The captain, smug in his belief that he had broken his spirit, did not note the flaming devils in the back of

El Halcon's eyes. Nor did he realize that those devils had sentenced him to death.

"All right," he growled. "No more out of you, or the next time you'll get fifty, or hung to the yardarm. That's what we do with mutineers. You signed up for a cruise, all ship-shape. Into the galley, now, and give the doctor a hand with the slops. Move!"

The glowering mate escorted Slade to the galley, where the "doctor," the ship's cook, presided. He was a wizened little man with squinty eyes.

"Here's a swab to give you a hand," said Parsons, the mate. "If he acts up, call me."

"Aye, aye, sir!" replied the doctor, scowling ferociously at Slade. "And I got a cleaver handy for the likes of him. All right, my man, get busy on them pots." He gestured to a big pan of steaming, soapy water. With an evil leer, the mate departed. Behind Slade the doctor cursed in a loud voice.

Abruptly he ceased his maledictions, slipped to the door and peered out. Slade was already busy with the dirty pots, trying to forget the stabbing pains in his back, and the volcanic wrath that strove to burst forth into action. Over his shoulder came the little doctor's whisper —

"Easy, Matey, take it easy. Just make it look like you're working in case that blankety-blank-blank bucko swab sticks his head in here again. Just a minute, let me look again."

Once more he peered out the door, came pattering back. "The so-and-so is busy and so are the rest of them," he breathed. "Quick, now, off with your shirt and let me get you careened for overhaul after them broadsides you took betwixt wind and water. You took 'em like a man, too. But you did well to trim your sails to the captain. If he wasn't so short-handed he would have killed you, and would have been within his rights according to the sea. Hitting the captain of a ship on the high seas is mutiny. Don't run afoul of him again. Him and his two bucko mates and that blankety-blank bo'sun will make pulp of you. Wait for a better time to even up. You got a head on your shoulders, matey, anybody can see that. Use it. Now let me get at that back with this slush — good slush, all grease, no salt. Make you feel a lot better."

The gnarled old hands were deft and gentle as a woman's. With his back well smeared, Slade felt a devil of a sight better. He donned his shirt. The doctor glanced out the door again, went to a cupboard and slipped out a bottle from a dark corner and filled a pannikin from it.

"Drink!" he ordered. "Good grog."

Slade obediently gulped down the contents of the pannikin, for his throat was like an oven; it was rum and water, plenty strong. He gagged a little from the fiery burn of it and the contraction sent a wave of pain through his back. That passed quickly, however, and as the liquor coursed through his veins, his condition continued to improve.

"That's better," said the doctor, with a keen glance at his face. "Now take old Peterby's advice. Batten down your hatch and obey orders. You're on a hell-ship, matey, and I ain't joshin'. Take it easy with them pots; you can't be in very good shape yet."

"If I don't wash them, you'll have to, won't you?" Slade asked.

"Guess I will," the doctor conceded.

"And I'm not in as bad shape as you might think," Slade added as he scoured away. "It wasn't pleasant, but it did me no real harm and jolted that poison I drank last night from my system. By the way, wasn't the captain in Corpus Christi commanding a steamer not long ago?"

"Guess he was," replied the doctor. "He transshipped at Blue Fields in Nicaragua. Same owner for both."

"Who's the owner?" Slade asked. The doctor shook his head.

"Dunno," he said. "Never heard his name called. Understand he owns quite a few, 'cording to the talk in the cabin I hear when I'm servin' those so-and-so's. Reckon this is the worst of the lot. Floggings like you got today, bad grub, poor pay. She's a hell-ship."

"Why do the men stand for it?" Slade asked. The doctor shrugged his scrawny shoulders.

"What can they do?" he countered. "They're a sorta scurvy lot. Drink too much. Ain't over bright. Can't get a berth on a really good ship. What can they do? Kill the blankety-blanks and take over the ship? What would they do with her? Couldn't make port and sooner or later a gunboat sending a ball athwart her bows as a hint to hove to. Then a ship with no papers. Next thing for them, a rope. Mutiny is mutiny, no matter if it is justified."

Slade thought a moment. He had been studying the doctor and had come to the conclusion that he was trustworthy and that his sympathy was genuine.

"Why do you stay on?" he asked. The doctor shrugged again.

"I'm old, and I don't look overmuch," he explained. "Not the sort a smart skipper will hire. And I ain't got it so bad. Good cooks ain't easy to come by and the captain and his mates like to eat. Besides, they know I'm a wee mite handy with a knife. And if a mate or a bo'sun comes up missing some fine morning, well, he fell overboard, that's all, and who's to say he might have been helped a mite to fall."

There was a cold gleam in the little man's squinty eyes as he spoke, eyes Slade noted were like splinters of sapphire in his weatherbeaten face. Yes, very likely the doctor was not a good man to impose on. He decided to play a hunch, although it might be risky to do so.

"Doctor," he said softly, "how would you like a berth on a really good ship with a really good captain?" For a third time the doctor shrugged.

"I'd like it," he conceded, "but there ain't much chance of me getting it."

Slade let the full force of his steady eyes rest on the other's face.

"It can be arranged," he said, even more softly.

The little man's eyes met his squarely.

"Do you mean it?"

"Yes, I mean it," Slade answered.

"And I reckon you can do it," the doctor muttered. "You ain't no sailor — you're a gent. I marked it when they brought you aboard last night. And I'm beginning to get a glim on this crazy cruise we made from Nicaragua. We didn't drop anchor in Corpus Christi. Stood off behind the island while the longboat went ashore with the mates and the bo'sun for cargo and some of the most worthless scuts aboard at the oars — they'd sell their own mothers for a bottle of grog. Matey, that boat went ashore on purpose to get you. Reckon they brought your mates along because the blasted scow was so short-handed and in no shape to weather the kind of blows that comes up all of a sudden in these waters. Yes, that was it, they were after you."

"Well, they got me," Slade said grimly. "What's the ship's name?"

"Right now she's the brig Ajax, but I reckon she's had quite a few names in her time. She's rotten. The hull's no good and neither are the sticks. Come a hard blow and they'll go by the board, watch what I tell you. The Ajax!"

The name struck a responsive chord in Slade's memory. Ajax! the mythical Greek hero who defied the lightning. Well, the Ajax, in the person of her captain, had defied the "lightning!" Which the captain would very likely realize before all was done.

"Any notion where we're bound for?" he asked.

The doctor again glanced around carefully before replying. "I hear talk in the cabin when I carry the kids to those so-and-so's," he replied. "I have to act steward, too, on this blasted scow. We're not bound for a port but to a beach somewhere in Central America, to pick up a load of contraband, guns most likely, for some of the Dons who figure to make trouble in Mexico. We'll land it up somewhere not far from the Texas coast, I'd say."

"I see," Slade said thoughtfully. "Doctor," he asked suddenly, "I was wearing my guns when I was brought aboard, wasn't I? Any notion where they are?"

"Yep, they're hanging on a hook in the captain's cabin, I saw 'em there this morning," the doctor replied. "Guns and belts, big ones."

Suddenly he cocked his head sideways and his voice rose in a harsh growl —

"All right, my man, get those slops overside. Move!"

As Slade picked up the two big pails, the mate stuck his head in the door, leered at him, sneered and departed.

Slade emptied the slops into the sea and returned to the galley. On his way he saw Norton and Shadwell holy-stoning the deck. Runt was not in evidence at the moment.

"Thought the blankety-blank would come nosing around and I was listening for him," said the doctor. He eyed Slade for a moment, dropped his voice to a whisper.

"Matey," he said, "if you aim to take the ship, take some advice. Don't try it till after she loads cargo and heads north again. You want to get out of Mexican waters first. If you run afoul of one of the Don's gunboats you'll be in trouble. Don't forget, now."

"I won't," Slade replied. "And I won't forget what I promised you, either, when the time comes."

"Guess you're the kind that doesn't forget," said the doctor. "By the way, my name's Peterby. What's yours?"

Slade supplied it and the doctor extended his hand. "What's the captain's name?" Slade asked as they shook.

"Jessup. The mate is Parsons. The second is Durling. The bo'sun, blast him! is Scully. Now I'll have to get busy with the cabin grub. I'll slip you a decent bite. By the way, your mates they brought along with you are seamen, aren't they? They look it."

"Yes, I guess they are, or have been," Slade answered.

"Then they'll know better than to buck the captain and the mates and will do their work and take what comes," predicted the doctor. "Look to be good men."

"They are," Slade said briefly.

When, hours later, thoroughly worn out, his back devilishly sore, Slade descended to the forecastle, he found Norton, Runt and Shadwell already there.

"Well, anyhow, we're all in the same watch, the mate's, and together," said the former. "I gather he always likes to take over the poor devils that are crimped and make life hell for them. Matey, what we going to do?"

"Right now," Slade replied in low tones, "we're going to wait. Our time will come. Obey orders, do your work and take all the abuse they hand out. At present there's nothing else to do."

Before the others of the watch, a grubby looking lot, put in an appearance, he outlined briefly his conversation with the doctor. The three listened eagerly.

"We'll make it and even up the score," Norton declared. "That is, if you're sure you can trust that cook."

"I'm sure," Slade replied.

"How's your back feel?"

"Not too bad," Slade answered. "Sore as the devil but no particular damage done. What the doctor put on helped a lot. And I've a notion they were careful not to cripple me for work."

"The lousy skunks!" growled Norton. "Just wait."

Slade nodded. "The mate's sadistic pleasure he derives from making life a hell for the crimped hands is liable to work against him this time," he remarked. "Being together off-watch will make it easier for us when the time comes. Right now all we can do is wait."

CHAPTER
TWELVE

During the days that followed, as the rotten old brig wallowed across the Gulf, bedeviled by contrary winds and often not making more than a knot or two an hour, Slade was handed all the dirty and humiliating jobs on the ship. He was given the morning chore of cleaning out the coops where chickens were kept for the consumption of the captain and his mates. He carried slops from the galley, did all the scullion work and shovelled out soot from the galley stove. He polished brass work and swept the officers' cabins. All this in what was supposed to be spare time.

Meanwhile he was learning seamanship. To this he applied himself avidly, knowing that the knowledge might come in mighty handy, later. He already knew something of the principles of sailing and worked fiercely to broaden his understanding of handling a ship. Within a very few days he could run aloft and do his trick of furling and clewing with the best of the forecastle men, including even Norton, Shadwell and Runt, who were experienced seamen of ability. Once he astonished them by sending down the skysail yard single-handed.

"Matey, you're all right," chuckled Norton. "You'll be a sailor before this infernal cruise is ended."

"Not much longer now, from what the doctor tells me," Slade said. "The northern coast of Honduras is where we're headed for, then pick up cargo and back north along the Mexican coast."

There came a night of wan moonlight and misty stars. The old brig nosed in cautiously toward a deep cove in the Central American coast. As she drew near, another ship, a schooner, was putting out. She was a thing of beauty, glistening with fresh paint, her new canvas towering banks of snow, flashing in the moonlight. Away she went under the thrust of the off-shore wind, heeling over, creaming her bows in the combers, her wake a phosphorescent sparkle.

"She delivered the stuff to the cove," old Peterby, the cook, said to Slade. "The owner don't risk her on the run to Mexico. Leaves that for this old tub."

"Same owner?" Slade asked.

"So I gather," said Peterby. "A beauty, ain't she?"

"She is," Slade returned thoughtfully, his black brows drawing together. Undoubtedly the owner was a man who kept his ships, some of them, in excellent shape. The Ajax and the tramp steamer, the Iago di Compostella, were evidently exceptions.

Slade gazed after the departing schooner, shadowy now against the blue-black waters of the Gulf. Abruptly some of his preconceived notions were getting a setback. If Rance Donner owned such a ship he sure kept the fact well hidden. He regretted that he could not catch her name; they were never close enough for that. However, he marked her well, every line and spar and fitting. He would know her if he saw her again.

The Ajax dropped anchor in the cove, minus riding lights. The buildings of a small town could be plainly seen, set back from the curving shore. All were dark.

The captain went ashore in the dinghy, Scully, the bo'sun, in charge of the boat crew.

All night long cargo was brought aboard by dark, barefooted men who wore steeple-crowned, broad-brimmed sombreros of woven straw. Hard, quiet men who spoke only when spoken to, and then in monosyllables. Till dawn the Ajax's crew labored incessantly, stowing away the heavy cases, until they were blind with weariness.

Captain Jessup was nervous and ill at ease, which increased his viciousness toward the crew, particularly Slade and his three companions. The mates and the bo'sun followed his lead, until it was all Slade could do to hold back the maddened trio.

"Wait," he said. "Don't spoil things by going off half-cocked. Wait till the doctor says we are at the right spot. He knows these waters and every inch of the Mexican coast. And we can trust him. Wait."

Twice the Ajax put in at sheltered coves and lay at anchor, hidden by near-tropical vegetation. And at night she carried no running lights.

"The old swab's scared he'll meet up with a gunboat with a nosy skipper," said Peterby. "No manifest for what he's carrying."

Then one day Peterby slipped Slade four long knives. "For you and your mates," he whispered. "I held onto 'em till the last minute, taking no chances they might be missed. Tonight's your night. Can't afford to wait any longer. They plan to kill you once the stuff's unloaded, you and your mates. Besides I don't like the looks of the weather over much. Got a notion something's building up in the Carribean, and if it is, we're liable to catch it. Steer a straight course and hit 'em between wind and water. I'll be right with you."

"The first mate's mine," said Shadwell.

"And I want the second," said Runt. "He kicked me in the ribs while I was holystoning the deck."

"Mine's the bo'sun," growled Norton, opening and closing his great hands. "Guess that leaves the captain to you, matey. Watch him, he'll be carrying his gun."

Slade nodded and said nothing.

While the captain, the mates and the bo'sun were eating dinner in the former's cabin, the mutineers struck. It was over in seconds. One sweep of Shadwell's knife nearly decapitated the first mate. Norton broke the bo'sun's neck with a single wrench of his great hands. Runt drove his blade under the second's ribs with an upward twist.

"Right where you kicked me, you blankety-blank!" he growled.

The captain managed to draw his gun, but Slade gripped his wrist before he could pull trigger. They wrestled mightily, slamming into chairs and the table. Back and back Slade bent the skipper's wrist. There was a flurry of exchanged blows, the hiss of labored breathing, while the others danced about unable to strike for fear of injuring Slade. Suddenly there was a flash and a boom. The captain gave a gurgling cry and sank to the deck, his throat torn open by the heavy slug. Slade stepped back, eyeing the corpse disgustedly.

"Accidently pulled the trigger and killed himself," he said. "Well, guess I had no business holding a grudge, anyhow, though he had it coming to him."

With a bound he crossed the cabin to where his cartridge belts and holsters hung from a hook. He buckled them on, made sure the big Colts were loaded.

The crew, aroused by the uproar, came boiling aft. But outside the door stood Peterby, the cook, with a knife in each hand.

"Belay there or I'll spill your guts all over the deck!" he bellowed.

Slade stepped through the door and drew both guns. "Back to your quarters," he told the sailors. "I'm captain of this ship now. Mr. Norton is first mate, Mr. Shadwell is second. Mr. Runt is bo'sun. You take orders from them from now on."

There was a confused murmur from the bewildered sailors. Norton strode forward.

"Stow that gab!" he roared. "You thought Parsons was a bucko mate, eh? Don't get *me* down on you or you'll think he was a lovin' sky pilot trying to make you happy. Now turn to and throw those carcasses to the sharks to pizen 'em, and make the captain's cabin shipshape! Move!"

"And Peterby," said Slade, "break out the captain's stores and cook a good meal for everybody and serve a tot of rum to all hands."

A cheer arose, and scowls turned to grins. Norton chuckled. "Better to have 'em with us than against us," he muttered.

114

Leaving Shadwell to superintend the tidying of the cabin, and Runt to keep an eye on the man at the wheel, Slade drew Norton aside.

"Chuck, now it's up to you to take hold," he said. "I'm no seaman as you very well know, although I've learned a good deal about it on this trip. I want you to head straight for the coast of Texas. No, not to Corpus Christi. Hit it somewhere east of Corpus Christi, if possible. We don't want to strike Padre Island. If a really bad blow comes, followed possibly by a tidal wave, the sea will very likely wash right over that hunk of sand and we'd all be drowned. I've a notion east of Corpus Christi Bay and west of Matagorda Bay will be your best bet. I know it's a bad coast there, but we're bound to hit somewhere if the weather gets really bad and I think we'll have the best chance with the mainland. Incidentally, I can navigate if necessary."

"Won't need any help if you just want to hit Texas," Norton replied. "I know these waters like the palm of my hand. And," he added soberly, glancing at the sky, "I figure the quicker we hit it the better. There's dirty weather coming or I'm bad mistaken, and this old scow is in no shape to tackle a Gulf hurricane with white squalls all of a sudden thrown in for good measure. A hard blow and she'll lose her sticks; they're rotten and worm eaten at the deck, and her hull won't stand any pounding. She should have been broken up in the yards long ago. Well, we haven't too far to go. What you going to do with her and the crew, Matey?"

"I'll think on that between here and the coast," Slade replied. "Right now I'm uncertain. It's something of a problem, but I'll work it out somehow. Well, I see they've got the cabin cleaned up. I'm going to have a look at the contents of the safe in there — glad the captain left it open; we might have had trouble breaking into it. May be able to learn something of interest from his papers."

Slade approached the safe with high hopes, but when, some time later, Norton entered the cabin, he found the Ranger staring at a heap of papers on the table and wearing a perplexed expression.

"Chuck," he said, "this is the queerest mess I ever cast eyes on. The manifest shows hides and tallow and everything appears ship-shape except for one thing. She's of Spanish registry, but wherever the ownership is mentioned, it's illegible, just a scrawl."

"Well," said Norton, "she really ain't much more than a pirate. She handles contraband, picking it up where other ships unload it, and things like that, so who wants to claim her. If the captain would have had to hove to and have his papers looked over, he'd give a phony ownership name and nobody could prove he wasn't right without a thorough investigation, and in *manana* land you can usually hush that up by slipping the right person a few pesos."

"Yes, I guess that's the explanation," Slade agreed. "As good as any I can think of, anyhow. Suppose you break open some of those cases in the hold and see what they contain."

"Already done it," Norton returned complacently. "Was curious and figured they might hold something we could make use of. Rifles, good ones, and

116

ammunition, just as the doctor figured. Consigned to *Dons* who have a mite of a revolution against old *El Presidente* Diaz in mind, I'd say."

"Very likely you're right," Slade conceded. "Well, the quicker we get to Texas the better. How's the weather."

"I don't like the looks of it," Norton replied. "I'm afraid there's a big blow been building up in the Carribean, and we're liable to catch it. Do the best we can, and that's all anybody can do, but we may get salt water over us till we're found pickled as herrings in a Swede fisherman's barrel. Here comes your dinner, and it's a good one. Mind if I eat with you? Runt and Shadwell are keeping an eye on things and the crew pears tame enough. Reckon they figure any change would have to be for the better."

Slade nodded. "By the way," he said, "there's quite a hefty helping of dinero in that pile over there on the corner of the table. Reckon the captain had it stashed away against an emergency. You and Shadwell and Runt and the doctor divide it among you; you've earned it. No, I don't want any of it. Divide it up among the four of you, I say."

"Guess we can use it," Norton chuckled as he stowed the sheaf of bills in his pocket. "Matey, you're all right."

As they ate the really excellent meal the doctor had thrown together on short notice, Norton suddenly cocked his head in an attitude of listening.

"Shadwell's shortening sail," he said. "He's getting the skies and the topgallants off her." A little later, "And the royals. Wind's freshening steadily, and she's rolling quite a bit more. Yep, I'm scairt we're in for trouble before the next twenty-four hours have passed. Not for a while, though, I predict. Better if it did come faster and blow itself out in a hurry. As it is, I've a notion there's a real ripsnorter cutting up in the Carribean and maybe veering westerly. If that's so, the Gulf'll catch blazes."

Their dinner finished, Slade and Norton went out onto the heaving deck. A wild white moon soared in the sky, with fragments of hurrying clouds. The Ajax was rolling heavily and the wind moaned in the cordage. Slade listened to the monotonous clank-clank of the pumps and gazed at the dark stream running through the scuppers.

"Is she taking much water?" he asked Shadwell.

"Not over much," the second replied. "But I'm trying to keep her dry against the chance that she'll be taking a lot more before long. This pounding is liable to open some seams. I'm afraid we're in for it."

Gazing at the tossing wave crests, Slade experienced an uneasy feeling that Shadwell was right. Sky and sea didn't look too good.

"Better get some sleep," Norton suggested. "I don't expect anything to worry about tonight. If it comes, it'll come some time tomorrow afternoon, I figure. When eight bells strike, and it ain't far off, I'll relieve Shad and let him turn in. See you tomorrow."

CHAPTER
THIRTEEN

Despite the wallowing of the old brig, Slade slept well. All in all, he was fairly pleased with developments although disappointed in not finding anything of importance in the captain's cabin. And after thinking the thing over, he was glad that he had not killed Captain Jessup; it would have been too much in the nature of a vengeance killing, of which he did not approve.

Awakening in the pale light of the dawn he went out onto the deck. The clouds had thickened and the whole vast expanse of the sky was a livid gray with flecks of wrack fleeing across it like startled birds still drunken from sleep. The wind had freshened still more and was blowing steadily from the southeast. The Ajax was carrying only a rag of canvas but was speeding north at a surprising rate.

All day long the wind steadily increased in violence. And ever and always, Chuck Norton gazed apprehensively southeast.

"It's coming," he muttered as the shades of evening began closing in. "Yes, it's coming, a real blow. Now what we've got to worry about is sudden squalls and we'll be mighty, mighty lucky if we don't get one. You see, in that big storm headed this way are winds up to a hundred and twenty miles an hour, whirling winds that send off blasts away from the center of the hurricane like jets of water from a bottle full of holes whirled around and around at the end of a spring. Those blasts develop into squalls with winds the devil alone knows how strong. If one hits us, this old tub will lose her sticks and maybe be pounded to pieces in no time. That's what we're up against, Matey, and we got to admit it."

It was not yet full dark and a lurid light overspread the raging sea when Slade noted a narrow line of black rising against the southern horizon.

"Looks like heavier cloud," he guessed to Norton.

"Uh-huh, but it ain't," the mate replied grimly. "That's wind, beating the sea up. We're going to catch it." His voice blared out like a thunderclap.

"All hands on deck to shorten sail! Leave her just enough for steering-way, Mr. Shadwell. Batten the hatches, clear the decks. Double lashings on everything. Mr. Runt, stretch a line from the fo'ks'l; another one from the galley. We'll need 'em. Move!"

The sailors worked madly to obey orders. Everybody lent a hand. Norton's gaze was fixed south. "Look out!" he shouted, perhaps twenty minutes later. "Here she comes!"

With a bellowing roar, a rattle of hailstones and a volley of rain the squall struck. The Ajax heeled over. Over and over, almost on her beam ends. The main mast snapped close to the deck and went overboard. The mizzen followed. The fore topmast tumbled slowly from the fidds and crashed across the deck in a sprawling litter of spars and cordage. The sailors cried their fright as they ducked and dodged to escape the falling stick. The splintered butts of the main and the mizzen pounded the ship's sides with shuddering blows.

"Clear the raffle!" boomed Norton. "Cut the lines 'fore those blasted sticks pound a hole in her!"

Slade led the attack, swinging an axe in the forefront, reeling and staggering on the slanting, slippery deck. Tons of green water frothed across the deck, threatening to sweep all overboard. The two men at the wheel spun the spokes madly, but the Ajax was little more than a helpless hulk, refusing to answer to her helm. She righted when she was freed of the slashing spars.

After a terrific battle against wind and water, a jury rig was gotten onto the stump of the foremast and the Ajax answered a bit better to the wheel.

For nearly thirty minutes the sea was an inferno of sound and fury. Then the squall passed. But the steady pressing wind from the southeast continued with added force.

The pumps were clanking, but Runt reported that she was taking little more water than before.

"Her hull's in better shape than I figured," he said. "I've a notion she'll stay afloat during the night. But when we near the coast —" His voice trailed off. No need to complete the sentence, which was very like a sentence of doom. Slade well knew that if the Ajax struck, and a tidal wave, as was not at all uncommon, followed the hurricane, the Ajax, or bits of her, would very likely be found a dozen miles out on the prairie.

On staggered the ship through the inky dark, battered, blasted, lurching, wallowing, her decks astream, her rag of canvas taut as a drumhead, but keeping on a fairly even keel. All sense of direction was lost, but the steady press of the wind gave Slade the course more surely than the wavering needle of the compass as he sought to plot their position by the dim glow of the binnacle. He knew that the hurricane would continue to come thundering out of the south by slightly east, and estimated that the wind was already blowing a good ninety miles an hour, with occasional gusts to much more.

"Anyhow, if we do strike, we'll strike just about where we planned to drop anchor," he observed to Norton. "Sort of cold comfort, under the circumstances, but something."

On and on the old Ajax plunged and wallowed, surrounded by pitch darkness and the storm. The gale roared above, with the peculiar tearing sound that accompanies the body of a hurricane; a sound suggestive of unbridled fury, as if elemental forces were ripping the envelope of the universe. The wind gained steadily in volume. It scooped the sea in steep ridges of solid water, flung the ship like a chip from crest to crest, or caught her, burst above her and swallowed her whole, as if she had suddenly sunk in a deep well. It was a night to turn the hair gray and shatter the mind.

Norton suddenly chuckled. "Smoke coming out of the galley," he said. "The doctor's got a fire going. That old coot could build a fire and cook under a waterfall. Something hot will sure help."

Peterby *had* gotten a fire going, and a huge boiler of coffee made, and an even larger one of lobscouse a-steam.

"Had to ballast 'em with a couple of links of anchor chain so they'd stay topside," he grinned.

Thankfully enough, bracing themselves against the bulkheads, the crew consumed the hot food and drink and returned to their labors in better spirits.

Norton glanced at the compass needle, squinted at the scrap of canvas dimly seen in the phosphorescent glow.

"She's holding, but I'm afraid the reefs will get her when we hit the coast," he remarked. "Reckon the owner's going to find himself short one."

The owner! Slade was struck by an idea. "See you in a minute," he told the mate and made his way along the line to the galley, where he found Peterby jammed against a bulkhead and calmly smoking his pipe.

"Pete," he said, "I believe you told me that the owner of this one is also the owner of the Iago di Compostella, that tramp steamer?"

"That's right," nodded Peterby. "I heard Jessup and the mate talking about it."

"And the Iago is Spanish registry, I think," Slade said thoughtfully. "Shouldn't be too hard to find out who owns her."

"Guess so," Peterby agreed. "Why?"

"Oh, just curious," Slade replied evasively. Peterby cast him a shrewd glance.

"Matey, you're a deep one," he said. "Sometimes I don't know what to make of you, but I reckon you've studied your chart and know the course you're sailing."

"I hope you're right," Slade answered, and returned to Norton.

Slade and his companions longed for, and dreaded the dawn, fearful of what they would see there to the north where the grim, broken coast of Texas and disaster waited. Even now they might be bearing down on it in the black darkness, with the boom of the breakers suddenly above the monotonous roar of the hurricane. They could only wait, and hope.

Finally a pale, watery light little by little crept into the east, disclosing a scene of utter terror. The face of the sea was livid with flying yellow foam; the torn sky hung closely over it like the fringe of a mighty waterfall. In the midst of this churning terror, the Ajax seemed momentarily on the point of disappearing, engulfed by the wrath of the elements.

And looming dark and threateningly close, terribly close, fringed by the deathly white of thundering breakers, was the coast of Texas!

"We're in San Antonio Bay, sure as shooting!" exclaimed Norton. "Been swept past the island and are headed for the mainland. Would have been better to strike the island. Now we're bound for the rocks. I thought I saw something loom on our portside last night but couldn't be sure. Matey, we're in for hell!"

In silence they gazed north. Then Slade said quietly,

"She's going to strike, and she'll go to pieces in no time. We'll have to take to the boats. God alone knows if we'll be able to make it, but we'll have to make the try; it's our only chance."

The other nodded agreement.

Slade went forward and called the crew together. "Get ready to abandon ship," he told them. "You fellows will go first in the longboat. The mates, the bo'sun, the doctor and myself will follow in the dinghy."

The sailors stared at him. One ventured, "Cap'n, you'll be taking an awful chance in that cockleshell."

"Perhaps," Slade conceded. "But there's no help for it. The longboat will accommodate you fellows, but it won't hold us all. Get ready; we're already dangerously close."

The longboat, loaded almost to capacity, swung in the davits. Norton, Shadwell, Runt and the doctor stood to the halyards. At Slade's signal, they hauled frantically. Slade spun the wheel. The wind spilled out, the Ajax came about and for an instant hung almost stationary.

"Lower away!" Slade roared.

Down went the longboat to strike the water with a resounding splash.

"They made it!" howled Runt. "Cast off! Cast off!"

Away went the longboat, her oars working frenziedly. "If the tackles had fouled or she'd slammed against the hull!" Shadwell muttered. "Didn't, though. Wonder if we can do as well."

"Let's go," Slade said. "Wait for what looks like a favorable moment, and let her slide."

By what seemed little short of a miracle, they made it and whisked away from the overhanging hull. Slade held the steering oar in an iron grip. The frothing breakers raced to meet them. The longboat was quite a bit ahead and going strong.

"One advantage of the dinghy, if she stays afloat, she draws less and can pass over something the longboat can't," Shadwell shouted above the bellow of the wind and the thunder of the breakers. "Another minute and we'll be in 'em."

Suddenly Runt gave a horrified cry. "There they go!" he yelled.

Glancing from the corner of his eye, Slade saw the bow of the longboat rear high. He heard no sound, but he knew she had struck a sunken reef. Up and up she went. The men were spewed into the sea like pips from a squeezed orange, to instantly vanish in the raging waters. The crew of the racing dinghy sat in numbed silence until Norton remarked in a hard, dry voice, "Well, anyhow, we won't be bothered about what to do with them."

Such was the Ajax crew's requiem as sung by Chuck Norton.

"And chances are we'll catch up with them before they reach Hades," added Peterby.

As they bore down on the breakers, Slade studied the sea ahead. His keen eyes saw a narrow lane of black and swirling water fringed on either side by the froth of deathly white. With all his strength he swung the oar till the dinghy's bow was pointed straight for that narrow path which was their only hope. The others bent their backs frantically to their oars to hold the little boat in line.

Into the maelstrom they swept. On either side the breakers raved and thundered. There was a grating beneath. The dinghy shuddered, seemed to slow. With the last atom of his strength, Slade fought the steering oar. Then behind them was the frightful roaring, ahead comparatively smooth water. A giant wave caught the dinghy on its crest and hurled it landward. With a crash it struck the beach. Its occupants were hurled to the sands. Bruised and bleeding they staggered to their feet, fighting the undertow of back-rushing water that threatened to sweep them to doom.

Runt fell. Slade seized his collar and, struggling through water waist-deep, hauled the half drowned man to safely. A dozen more staggering steps and he paused.

"This had ought to do it for the moment," he croaked. "Rest a bit and then start going again. We've got to get out of reach of the possible tidal wave."

He seized Runt about the waist and shook most of the salt water out of him and set him on his feet. The bo'sun grinned wanly.

"Thanks, matey," he gasped between retchings. "Thought I was headed for Davey Jones' locker sure as shootin'."

"Here comes the Ajax!" exclaimed Shadwell. "She's going to strike!"

Even above the roar of the wind and the sea they heard the crash. Then the old brig lay surging and wallowing, ground in the iron jaws of the reefs.

"She'll break up in minutes," muttered Norton.

127

Slade nodded and turned away; it is not pleasant to watch a ship die.

"Where do you figure we are, Chuck?" he asked.

Norton studied the coast. "Nigh forty miles east of Corpus Christi, I'd say," he replied.

"That's my estimate," Slade agreed. "And if so there should be an east-west trail a few miles to the north. We'll make for it. How you feeling, Runt?"

"I'm okay now I've got the blasted Gulf of Mexico out of me," the other replied with a wan grin. "Let's go!"

As they got under way, Norton asked, "What we going to tell 'em in Corpus Christi?"

"The truth," Slade replied, "that we were crimped, as I guess they know by now, that the ship hit the reefs and sank with us the sole survivors. No need to mention anything else just yet."

"That's right," agreed Norton, the others nodding assent. "Mutiny is mutiny, from the way the owners look at it, and if what happened got around it might be brought against us if we took a notion to ship out again. But what if the owner gets to nosing around trying to find out just what did happen?"

"I wish he would," Slade said grimly, "but he won't."

Norton glanced at him inquiringly, but Slade did not choose to elaborate at the moment.

The destruction of the Ajax appeared to be the storm's final effort, for the wind steadily decreased in violence.

"We didn't catch the center of it," said Norton. "Be calm after a bit, and then we may get some wind from the other direction, but not much."

This was brush country and the going was hard, but they pushed on doggedly and, as Slade predicted, after a while they struck a trail and turned west.

"Well, this is better," said Norton, stretching his legs. "Got quite a cruise ahead of us, though."

"We should strike a ranchhouse somewhere along here, and there we may be able to pick up horses," Slade told him.

As Slade expected, a few miles farther on they spotted a *casa* set back from the trail. Several cowhands loitering about under the clearing sky stared in astonishment as the bedraggled quintet trudged wearily into the yard. A man standing on the veranda let out a bellow.

"Ain't you jiggers got sense enough to stay in out of the rain?" he demanded. "Come on in, come on in and dry out."

The invitation was gratefully accepted. The owner gave Slade a keen glance.

"Cowhand, aren't you?" he asked.

"When I'm working at it," Slade replied. "Right now I feel more like a duck."

The rancher chuckled. "What happened?" he asked.

"Ship we were on was driven onto the reefs and sunk," Slade told him. "We're the sole survivors."

The rancher clucked sympathetically. "I'm Jess Crane and this is the Cross C spread," he announced. Slade supplied his own name and introduced his companions.

"Slade," repeated Crane as he shook hands. "Seems to me I've heard that name somewhere not long ago."

Slade tried a long shot. "Happen to know Clark Kendal?"

"Sure," Crane replied. "Known him for forty years, friend of mine. Do you know — hey! I've got you placed! Slade! You're the feller who saved his little gal from getting burned up! Slade, I'm mighty, mighty glad to know you!"

He crossed to an inner door and gave a whoop, "Hot coffee and chuck on the table, pronto!" He turned back to Slade.

"Heading for Corpus Christi?"

"That's right," El Halcon nodded. "And I was wondering if we could borrow some cayuses to finish the trip?"

"Sure," answered Crane. "I have some old plugs the sea fellers can ride, and I reckon you can fork anything with four legs. Now take it easy, you fellers, you look plumb tuckered. You'll squat here tonight. There's room for your boys in the bunkhouse and I'll bed you upstairs, Slade."

That night Slade told Crane as much of their adventures as he thought advisable. The rancher swore and shook his head.

"Don't know what that blasted town's coming to," he growled. " 'Pears nobody is safe. What they need there is some Rangers."

Slade did not comment.

"A couple of my boys will ride in with you, to bring back the horses," Crane added. "Now you hit the hay; you need rest."

CHAPTER
FOURTEEN

Upon arriving at Corpus Christi the following morning, Slade turned the horses over to the Cross C hands and at once repaired to the waterfront.

"What I need right now is a noggin of rum," said Norton. "Coming with us, Slade?"

"First I want to see Badding," Slade replied.

"Okay," said Norton. "We'll see you at the office after we splice the main brace. Come on, Pete."

Slade paused at the livery stable to visit Shadow, who greeted him with a disgusted snort that seemed to say, "Off on a drunk, eh?"

But the way he thrust his velvety muzzle into Slade's hand and blew softly belied his sarcasm.

"Was wondering what to do with him when you didn't show up," said the keeper. "But Cock Badding came around and told me to keep him here till he died of old age if necessary and that he'd bust my neck if I didn't. I figured he meant it."

"Wouldn't be surprised if he did," Slade smiled reply. "Thanks for taking such good care of him; he looks fine."

"Needs to stretch his legs," replied the keeper. "Okay otherwise. Be seeing you."

Cock Badding stared in astonishment at the bearded, unkempt figure that strode into his office. Then he let out a joyous whoop.

"Slade!" he bellowed. "Where the devil did you come from? Is this the Resurrection Day ahead of schedule?"

"Hardly think so, but I came close to taking the first step in that direction," Slade answered as they shook hands.

"Sit down and tell me about it," said Badding.

Slade did so, to the accompaniment of growls and oaths from the labor contractor.

"I learned you'd been crimped, of course," said Badding when Slade paused. "When you and the boys didn't show up I got suspicious and began tracing your movements. At that rumhole down the street, which has a reputation for such things, I threatened to kill a few people and got the truth, or part of it. All they knew, or would admit to knowing, was that a bunch of hellions came in and packed you off while you were sleeping, saying they'd take care of you. Of course the infernal bartender and the waiter were in on it, but there's no proving it and they weren't around when I was there. A lubber said he saw the four of you dumped into a longboat. To tell the truth I never expected to see any of you alive again and I've been trying to figure some way to even the score. Now what?"

"First a shave and some clothes," Slade replied.

"Then you'd better ride over to Clark Kendal's spread and let him know you're all right," said Badding.

"He was here, and he acted like a madman. Said he was going to wire the capital, and Washington, and have the whole blasted U.S. Navy hunting for you. The little gal's eyes were red, like she'd been crying. Yes, you'd better hustle over there pronto."

He drew money from a drawer and handed it to Slade. "Your wages," he explained. "You've been on the payroll all the time of course. Now don't argue. That's the way I want it and that's the way I'm going to have it."

Without argument, Slade accepted the money, realizing that Badding would feel hurt if he didn't.

"By the way," he said, "do you think you could learn who owns that tramp steamer, the Iago di Compostella?"

"Reckon I could," replied Badding. "Shouldn't be too hard. Yes, I'll find out."

"You may have to dig through some holding company or two," Slade said.

"Don't worry, I have my ways of doing things," Badding assured him. "I'll find out."

"I'd take it as a big favor if you do," Slade said. Badding shot him a keen glance, but asked no questions.

While they were still talking, Norton and others arrived. Badding solemnly shook hands with Peterby.

"You're going to my place to rest up for a week or two, old feller, then I'll get you a good berth on a good ship if I have to call a general waterfront strike to do it," Badding declared.

After making himself presentable, Slade dropped in at the sheriff's office. Cole greeted him warmly but was less surprised than Badding had been.

"Oh, I knew you'd come out on top, no matter what tangle you'd gotten yourself into, you always do," he said. "But it sure looks like they're after you, all right."

"Yes, they laid a trap for me and I blundered right into it," Slade replied. "I'd had warning enough that they were watching my every move. When we stopped at that rumhole it gave them their chance. Norton and the others were too drunk to remember the reputation the place had or were in a condition to not give a darn for anything. I should have known better. Well, I have a few scars on my back to remind me of my carelessness."

"The ornery hyderphobia skunks!" growled the sheriff, when Slade paused after concluding his narrative. "They got exactly what was coming to them."

"Only the fact that the skipper was very short-handed saved us," Slade added. "Otherwise we'd have been dumped in the Gulf without delay. He took a chance, thinking he'd broken our spirit with his brutality, and kept us alive for a while, planning to do for us as soon as he'd unloaded his contraband cargo. That's where he slipped a mite, as the owlhoot brand always does sooner or later. All you have to do is keep alive long enough."

"Under certain circumstances a pretty large order," the sheriff commented dryly. "Got any notion who's back of it all?"

134

Slade shook his head. "No," he admitted, "but I do have a little something to work on. The ownership of that steamer, for instance. Old Peterby insists that the owner of the steamer and the owner of the brig are the same. And I got a very good look at the schooner that delivered the contraband cargo to the beach; I'll recognize her if I see her again."

"Which is something," conceded Cole. "Now what you going to do?"

"Now I'm going to ride out to Clark Kendal's spread," Slade replied.

"A good notion, before he busts a cinch," nodded the sheriff. "He was in to see me and he acted as if he was going loco. Yes, that's a good notion."

Several cowhands doing chores around the barn recognized Slade when he rode into the ranchhouse yard, and shouted a welcome. One came hurrying to take charge of Shadow and after a word from Slade the big black followed him docilely to the barn.

Aroused by the commotion, old Clark and Gay appeared in the doorway. The rancher let out a joyous bellow. Gay fairly threw herself in his arms.

"Finest surprise I've had in a coon's age," Kendal declared. "Come on in and tell us what the devil you got yourself into."

Slade told them everything, feeling that it was to his advantage to do so. Gay shuddered as the tale progressed and her eyes blazed with anger. Old Clark looked grave.

"'Pears you've made yourself some mighty bad enemies," he observed.

"Yes, looks that way," Slade conceded.

"And the El Halcon yarn is getting results."

"It looks that way," Slade repeated.

"Why in the world do you allow such a story to go around?" Gay demanded indignantly.

"Once such things start they're hard to stop," Slade replied evasively.

"I dropped in to see Cole and mentioned it," old Clark observed, looking reminiscent.

"What did he have to say?" Slade asked.

"He said he reckoned if a man was born a darn fool he usually stayed that way all his life; and he wasn't referring to you."

Slade shook with laughter. "The sheriff's all right," he said.

"Always was and always will be," Kendal agreed. "Well, it's time to eat and I'm hungry. How about you?"

"After that starvation cruise I don't think I'll ever get filled up again," Slade answered.

"Going to stay over night, of course?"

"Of course," Slade said, with a glance at Gay, who smiled and blushed.

Kendal tugged his mustache thoughtfully. "You told Cole everything?"

"Cole and Badding," Slade replied. "We decided it was better not to put out for general consumption what happened to the captain and his mates."

"A good notion," agreed Kendal. "No sense in making talk and getting folks to wondering and asking questions. Let the hellions back of it do a little guessing

136

as to just what did happen. Well, there's the cook bellerin'; let's go eat.

"I got to find him a helper," he added irrelevantly, apropos of the cook. "He's getting old and this is a big outfit. But good cooks ain't easy to come by."

Slade suddenly had an inspiration. "Mr. Kendal, do me a favor and don't hire another cook till you hear from me," he requested. "I've got somebody in mind who will be just the man for you, if I can persuade him to take a job."

"Who?" Kendal asked.

"Old Peterby, the Ajax cook," Slade replied. "I figure it's time he settled down ashore, and he's a darn good cook."

"The feller who helped you so much, eh?" said Kendal. "Fine! fine! Bring him along. Be mighty, mighty glad to have him. I figure I owe him plenty."

"Yes, plenty," Gay seconded the invitation. "Try and get him to come here, Walt."

Just as dusk was falling, the Tumbling K had another visitor. A grotesque figure with absurdly shortened stirrups rode into the yard. However, Hayes Wilfred swung from the saddle lithely enough and mounted to the veranda with assured steps. He had evidently heard of Slade's escape for he greeted him without surprise.

"We were beginning to fear we'd lost you, Mr. Slade," he said. "I gather you had a quite thrilling adventure."

"I imagine a Gulf hurricane is always a bit thrilling," Slade answered noncommitally.

"Yes, even under ordinary circumstances, but more so I would say when one is forced to face one contrary to his inclinations. You have no idea who was responsible for you being shanghaied?"

"The ship was very short-handed," Slade replied. "I understand that crimping is not altogether uncommon in this section."

"Too common," said Wilfred. "A despicable practice. Handle a ship as it should be handled and there is no need to resort to it. But I fear we have owners along the Coast who will stoop to anything for profit."

"They'd look fine dancing at the end of a rope," growled Kendal. "Did you want to see me about those shipments, Hayes?"

"Yes, if you have the time to spare," Wilfred said.

"You'll excuse us, won't you, Slade?" said Kendal. "We got some business matters to go over. Come into the office, Hayes, and we'll straighten things out."

He led the way to the room he used for an office and closed the door, leaving Slade and Gay alone.

"Seems to be a rather nice sort," Slade remarked apropos of the ship owner.

"I think he hates me," Gay said slowly.

"Why?"

"Because he asked me to marry him."

Slade grinned. "As a rule that is not a way to express hate," he demurred.

"But I refused him," Gay said. "Oh, it is not because I refused him but because he is convinced that I did so because of his deformity. That had nothing to do with it. If I'd cared for him that way it would have meant

138

nothing to me. I've known him a long time and unless he calls attention to it I never think of it. I just never cared for him particularly. Why I really can't say. A woman's intuition, perhaps. He's been Dad's friend for several years and he is cultured, educated, and wealthy. And he can be very charming; and his face is strikingly handsome, don't you think?"

"Yes."

"But there always seems to be something hard and ruthless in his nature," the girl went on. "I understand he has a terrible temper, and he is frightfully strong. I've heard that once he killed a man with his hands, a man who laughed at his legs."

"He doesn't appear to be sensitive about it," Slade observed thoughtfully.

"So it seems, but I'm not so sure," Gay said. "He jokes about it, but I don't think it would be safe for anybody else to joke about it."

"Evidently," Slade agreed dryly.

"No, it was not because of his deformity that I refused him," Gay repeated. "Of course it's fine for a man to be tall and straight but if a woman really cares for a man, that would be far from the most important thing. However, I fear there's no convincing Hayes Wilfred of the truth. I can sense his hate, and sometimes I'm just a little afraid of him."

"I really don't think you have any reason to be," Slade said.

"Perhaps not, but the feeling is there and I can't altogether banish it, though I tell myself I'm just being foolish and imagining things. And I really don't think I'm exactly the scary sort."

"You have demonstrated that several times to my knowledge," he smiled. "Even being marooned with a man on a lonely beach at night didn't faze you."

"Oh, I was plenty scared — scared that you'd ignore me."

"I didn't."

"No, you certainly did not." With a reminiscent glow in her big eyes. "And I hope you never will."

"I won't."

"And I'll always be a pleasant memory?"

"Why just a memory?"

"Because, my dear, that's all a woman means to you — a memory. You see, I'm not fooling myself one bit. Oh, well, it's nice to be at least — a memory."

The appearance of old Clark and Hayes Wilfred ended a conversation that had continued long enough, for the time being.

"Sorry, Clark, but I've got to get back to town tonight," Wilfred was saying. "I have a ship sailing with the tide and I want to be there when she puts out. Yes, I'll have a snack and coffee before I go, if it isn't too much trouble."

"I'll take care of it," Gay volunteered. "I think Stiffy has gone to the bunkhouse for a card time." Stiffy was the cook.

As they sat with Wilfred at table, Slade studied the man and arrived at the conclusion that Gay was probably right when she said there was a certain hardness and ruthlessness in Hayes Wilfred's make-up.

140

Not particularly surprising, though, the Ranger thought. A man born with such a handicap might well develop an antagonistic attitude toward others. Hayes Wilfred, by his own fierce energy, had overcome what could have floored another man and rendered him incompetent. He had gained a position of power and affluence. And such are seldom acquired without firmness and a driving force that his opposition often maintains is a callous disregard for the rights of others. Men successful in any line of endeavor are not often of the shrinking violet type.

All of which Walt Slade was wont to view with tolerance and understanding. He admired Hayes Wilfred for his achievements in the face of what appeared to be insurmountable difficulties. And yet he was forced to agree with Gay Kendal that the man lacked warmth, although that could also mean but an inner sensitiveness that he suppressed and refused to let appear on the surface for fear it might be misunderstood as a seeking for sympathy. Something that a man of his character would bitterly resent.

Later, they watched him ride away through the moonlight, his huge shoulders squared, his magnificently shaped head held high. Slade regarded the set of the shoulders, the poise of the head with an expression of slight perplexity.

"Now who the devil does *he* remind me of?" he wondered. "Seems there's always somebody looking like somebody else in this blasted section!" His glance dropped to the small girl beside him. Well, anyhow she didn't look like anybody else he'd noticed so far. She

141

was strictly herself, and a very lovely self. His arm was around her trim waist when they mounted the stairs together.

CHAPTER
FIFTEEN

Cock Badding had insisted that he take a good rest before returning to work, so Slade spent a couple of very pleasant days at the Tumbling K ranchhouse. Riding over the ranch with Gay, he was impressed at the excellence of the holding. Clark Kendal was a cattleman, all right.

When he returned to Corpus Christi, he paused at the sheriff's office before repairing to the waterfront. He found there an elderly dark-faced gentleman with a pleasant expression, who spoke perfect though precise English.

"Slade," said the sheriff, "I want you to know Senor Sebastian Alvarez, a land owner of Mexico and who's been my *amigo* for a lot of years. *Senor*, you may speak freely before Slade."

"Assuredly," said the other, acknowledging the introduction with a courtly bow. "I have heard of him; who has not? El Halcon, the friend of the lowly!

"As I was saying," he continued, "I am gravely concerned over the flow of contraband arms into my country. Arms that will be put to no good use."

"Yes," nodded Cole, "but that's hardly in my province; preventing the smuggling is a chore for the Customs people."

"Agreed," said Alvarez, "but because of the activities men have been murdered on Texas soil, and that *is* in your province."

"That I won't argue," replied the sheriff.

"Do not misunderstand me," said Alvarez. "I do not approve of the so-called 'Land Reforms.' My sympathies are with the *peons*, the humble people of the soil. The time will come when a real patriot will arise and right their wrongs, but that time is not yet. What is misnamed a revolution will be nothing more than organized and well financed banditry. Only the promoters of the movement will benefit. The people will not. There will be murder, robbery, pillage. Ultimately the iron hand of *El Presidente* oppressing the people even more heavily than at present. Unfortunately there are misguided men of my own status who are being duped into taking part in the movement; they pay heavily for smuggled arms, without which the movement cannot get underway. When *El Presidente* acts, and he will act, the people will suffer and the leaders will escape with their ill-gotten gains. Nor will Mexico alone suffer. The Border will be aflame and the fire will leap the Great River to Texas soil, with attendant bloodshed and depredations. If the flow of arms continues, what I have outlined is inevitable."

Slade spoke for the first time. "And you believe that Corpus Christi is the focal point of the smuggling?"

"It is, of that I am positive," replied Alvarez. "Here is the smugglers' headquarters. Who are they? That I do not know. I don't even know whom to suspect. That is why I have appealed to my old *amigo*, the sheriff."

144

"He won't let you down," Slade said. Alvarez smiled.

"Of that I am assured," he said. "Also, now that El Halcon is here, I am assured that soon all will be well."

"I hope your confidence won't be misplaced," Slade answered.

"It will not be," Alvarez stated positively. "*Senores*, I came here greatly perturbed. Now I am in a most complacent frame of mind. *Adios!*"

"Alvarez is okay, and I've a notion he's got the situation sized up about right," said the sheriff, after the rancher had departed.

"He has," Slade agreed. "And to make matters more interesting, it would appear that somebody is or was trying to horn in on the smuggling monopoly. The blowing up of that ship the day I arrived here tends to corroborate the belief. That explosion was black powder, not dynamite. I've a notion somebody set a match to her contraband cargo, with the result that men died on what is Texas soil. Which gives us ample reason for going deeply into the matter. Well, I don't appear to be making much headway, but sometimes things work out unexpectedly. Perhaps I'll get a surprise."

He was due to get one, very shortly.

Cock Badding was at his desk when Slade reached the office. "Well, I got your information for you," he said, after they had greeted each other, shoving a sheet of paper to Slade. "The Iago di Compostella was bought by the man whose name is on that paper, eight years ago. She retained her Spanish registry and was

145

put in the Pacific islands trade. Only showed in these waters recently."

Slade stared at the name. "Badding, are you sure?" he said. Badding nodded. Slade continued to study the paper.

"Where was the sale consummated?" he asked.

"At New Orleans."

"Perhaps something relative to the owner could be learned there," Slade remarked.

"Quite likely," nodded Badding. He shot Slade a curious glance.

"Walt, why are you so interested in this business?" he asked.

"They tried to kill me, didn't they?" Slade returned.

"Guess they did," Badding conceded, looking not at all satisfied with the explanation that didn't explain. "What do you think of it?"

"To tell the truth, I don't know what to think, yet," Slade replied slowly.

Which was so, for the name written on the paper was —

"J. W. Donner"!

Cock Badding spoke: "Looks like Rance Donner's your man, eh?"

"Yes, Cock," Slade replied. "It looks that way. In fact, it looks too darn much that way."

"What do you mean by that?"

"I mean I have learned to distrust the obvious."

146

Again there was silence. Then Badding leaned forward, his eyes steady, his voice earnest.

"Walt," he said, "I'm your friend. You know I can be discreet, and that I'll help you in any way I can. Won't you tell me just who you are and what you are, and why you're here? Don't you think you can trust me?"

"Yes," Slade answered, arriving at a decision and fumbling with his belt. "Yes, I think I can." He laid something on the table between them.

Cock Badding stared at the famous silver star set on a silver circle.

"So that's it," he muttered. "I might have known it. And you're here to clean up this mess, eh?"

"I'm here to try and clean it up," Slade corrected. "So far all I've been able to do is try."

"You'll do it," Badding declared. "No doubt in my mind as to that. But to get back to Donner. Maybe Rance Donner isn't the one. Maybe there are two Donners in the shipping business. It's not exactly an uncommon name."

"Yes, but all the circumstances considered, I feel that would be stretching coincidence a mite too far," Slade replied. "By the way, how does Rance Donner sign his name?"

"R. H. Donner."

"No help there; I thought maybe he might use a W. Anyhow, it —"

At that moment, the man they had been discussing entered the office; and if the warmth of Rance Donner's greeting was assumed, Slade felt he was one of the finest actors that never trod the boards.

"So you made it back safely," Donner said. "Mind telling me just what happened? I got what was doubtless a garbled version in the bars."

Slade told him, briefly, refraining from mentioning the fate of the captain and his mates. He thought he sensed a shadow crossing Donner's eyes and a slight tightening of his lips when he mentioned the name of the brig. Although he was not sure but that he imagined it.

"The Ajax," Donner repeated. "And she broke up on the reefs. I suppose there was nothing left of her worth salvaging."

"Highly unlikely, I would say," Slade replied. "There was a terrific surf and she was doubtless ground to pieces and the fragments of her cast far and wide."

Donner nodded soberly. "Well, I'm mighty, mighty glad that you came out of it with a whole skin, which is more than we expected when we heard what had happened. This port is getting worse by the day. I've half a mind to transfer my activities to Galveston or some place where there is something resembling peace, although Corpus Christi is a very advantageous port most of the time. Well, perhaps things will quiet down after a bit; I certainly hope so. Badding, I can use an overtime crew tonight if you can get one together for me."

"I'll get one," Badding promised. He watched Donner's tall form pass through the door, a speculative gleam in his eyes.

Slade also watched the ship owner depart and once again he was plagued by the feeling that he greatly resembled somebody he had contacted not long before. And once again he was baffled when he tried to recall just who the elusive somebody possibly could be.

"Well," remarked Badding when he was sure Donner was out of hearing. "Well, it looks like he might be getting ready to pull out, judging from what he just said. Maybe he figures things are getting a mite hot hereabouts and that he'd better up anchor and away before it begins to blow great guns. You know he can't be sure just how much you might have learned about that blasted ship."

"Not beyond the realm of possibility, but, I feel, improbable," Slade returned. "Cock, somehow the jigger just doesn't fit into the picture, although I may be making a serious mistake."

"If not him, who?" Badding asked. "Anybody else you got your eye on?" Slade shook his head.

"That's the devil of it, he said. "There's not one person I've contacted or heard mentioned that does fit into the picture. I'll have to admit that right now if Donner is discarded, I'm up against a stone wall so far as suspects are concerned. Oh, well, maybe I'll get a break."

"More likely you'll make one," said Badding. He began to laugh softly. Slade glanced at him in surprise.

"El Halcon a Texas Ranger!" he chortled. "If that don't take the paint off the smoke stack! Does anybody here besides me know it?"

"Only the sheriff, I hope," Slade replied.

"Cole's all right," said Badding, "but I'm afraid the situation here is too much for him to handle. He's like the majority of his class, a cowhand who got elected. Fast with a gun, honest, dependable, but lacking in training. Isn't that about it?"

"Just about," Slade conceded. "And I'm beginning to think that I'm lacking in training or something, judging from the progress I'm not making."

"Oh, you'll come out on top," Badding predicted cheerfully. He grinned.

"But seeing as you're still working for me, suppose you mosey out and get Donner's crew together," he suggested. "Give you a chance to rest your mind."

Slade was indeed glad to get out and occupy himself with something humdrum for a while. His mind was really in a good deal of turmoil. Not only the unexpected result of Badding's investigations had upset him. The conversation with *Don* Sebastian Alvarez had given him cause for grave concern. An abortive uprising in Mexico might well bode serious consequences for the Texas Border country. At the very least, the section would be overrun by streams of fleeing refugees seeking sanctuary north of the Rio Grande. Which would be resented by the Border dwellers and very likely there would be bloodshed and other depredations. It had happened before and might well happen again. Which the Ranger earnestly hoped to avert. And it appeared that the only way to avert such a tragedy was to stop the flow of contraband arms into Mexico. That was his real problem and it seemed he was no nearer a solution than when he arrived in the two-tiered town. Not altogether, however; he still had a couple of leads which might burgeon some tendrils that would weave the web of intrigue into a readable pattern.

On the way to the pier where Donner's ship was moored, he passed the saloon from which he and his companions were shanghaied; he paused in astonishment.

The swinging doors were torn off. The windows were smashed. The unlighted interior was a shambles of splintered furniture, and the place appeared to be deserted. Slade chuckled and passed on. Evidently the boys had taken care of the joint properly.

Slade was only momentarily surprised. The longshoremen, most of them former sailors, were a rough and ready lot and resented such shenanigans, especially when men as popular as Norton, Shadwell and Runt were the victims of the outrage, and when they expressed their displeasure they did it wholeheartedly. There would be no more crimping from *that* place.

When Slade located Norton and his two cronies, they gave him an uproarious greeting. Nearby, old Peterby sat on a barrel watching them work.

"Funny thing happened at that place where we were crimped," Norton observed. "Just about closing time a bunch of jiggers from somewhere or other went in there and plumb tore the place apart. Busted the barkeep's head with a bottle. Oh, they didn't kill him; just bloodied him up a bit. Funny thing to do, wasn't it?"

"Fellows do funny things sometimes when they're drinking," Slade replied. "Guess they didn't like the barkeep's face."

"Well, it's sorta different now from what it was before they got through with him," Norton chuckled. "Sure we'll work overtime tonight. I sent most of that dinero to my mother and I can use a few extra pesos. Pier six at eight o'clock? We'll be there, and the boys will come with us. Be seeing you."

Norton went back to work and Slade accosted Peterby.

"Pete," he said, "I figure it's about time you settled down ashore. How'd you like to be a ranch cook? There'll be another man in the kitchen and you can learn things about new dishes from each other."

"Matey, I'd like it fine," Peterby answered gratefully. "After that last voyage, I sort of don't hanker to ship out again. It's a dog's life at best, and I ain't young any more."

"Okay," Slade said. "We'll ride out there in a few days. You'll find Mr. Kendal a fine man to work for."

After knocking off until the night chore, Slade repaired to the telegraph office, where he sent a wire addressed to Captain Jim McNelty at Ranger Post headquarters —

"Learn what you can concerning one J. W. Donner ship owner. Was located in New Orleans eight years ago."

He regarded the operator steadily as he handed him the message. "Be sure that your company's rule forbidding the divulgence of the contents of any message sent over the wires is obeyed," he said.

"It will be, especially on this occasion," the operator promised emphatically.

152

"Should be an answer some time tomorrow," Slade said. "Hold it for me."

Donner's cargo — hides, tallow and other harmless merchandise — was loaded without incident. Slade had a drink with Chuck Norton and his bunch went to bed. At noon the following day he visited the telegraph office and found an answer from Captain Jim awaiting him. His black brows drew together as he perused it and he shook his head.

Returning to Badding's office, he handed him the telegram.

"Well, I'll be hanged!" growled the labor contractor as he read —

"J. W. Donner died suddenly in New Orleans six years ago. Will try to learn more concerning him."

Badding looked up from the paper to meet Slade's gaze. "And what the devil does *this* mean?" he wondered.

"Your guess is as good as mine," Slade answered. "Maybe Captain Jim can dig up something helpful."

"Everything 'pears to be getting no better fast," grunted Badding. "Now I don't know what to think about that jigger. One thing is sure for certain, *he* isn't J. W. Donner who bought the Iago di Compostella."

"If he is, he's done a mighty fast job of reincarnation," Slade said.

"He's a fast worker, all right, but I don't think he's that fast," said Badding.

CHAPTER
SIXTEEN

Several uneventful days followed. Slade delivered Peterby to the Tumbling K ranchhouse, where he was warmly received.

"Matey," he said to Slade, later, "I think I got a home. It was sure a fine day for me when that blankety-blank-blank mate shoved you into my galley."

"It was a fine day for me, too," Slade told him. "Otherwise, I might not be here today."

Old Peterby glanced at Gay, who was lending a hand in the kitchen.

"And Matey, I think you got a home here, too, if you want it," he chortled. "That would make things just perfect."

"You may have something there," Slade smiled.

Three days later a ship entered Corpus Christi Bay, a beautiful schooner, her towering canvas snowy-white, her hull and deck houses gleaming with fresh paint. Slade watched her approach, his black brows drawing together until the concentration furrow was deep between them, a sure sign that El Halcon was doing some hard thinking.

The schooner's shining sails fluttered down, one by one, like wounded birds, and she eased gently to her pier.

"Cock," Slade said to Badding, who stood beside him, "who owns that vessel?"

"That's the Orpheus, one of Hayes Wilfred's fleet," Badding replied. "Why?"

Slade turned to face him. "Cock," he said, "that is the ship I saw leaving the Honduras cove the night the Ajax loaded contraband arms for Mexico!"

Badding's eyes widened. "Walt, are you sure?" he demanded.

"Yes, I'm sure," Slade replied. "That's her; I marked her well and knew I'd recognize her if I saw her again. Well, I'll be hanged!"

"What the devil does it mean?" asked Badding.

"I'd say," Slade answered grimly, "that it means *Señor* Hayes Wilfred is doing a little gun running, and perhaps some other things that won't bear the light of day."

"Wh-what you going to do, drop a loop on him?" Badding sputtered.

"For what?" Slade countered. "For owning a ship? I am convinced in my own mind that the Orpheus is the ship I saw putting out from the cove, but I couldn't prove it. A ship I saw at a distance by moonlight. And it is only surmise on my part that she left the contraband cargo there to be picked up by the Ajax. I didn't see her leave it. You can't make a case that will stand up in court out of such evidence. I'd just make a laughing stock of myself. *This* is going to require a bit of thinking out."

"Well, anyhow, it looks like you've got somebody besides Rance Donner to keep an eye on," Badding said.

"Yes," Slade agreed thoughtfully. "Somebody besides Rance Donner."

With Badding occupied with some matters on the piers, Slade walked back to the office and sat down, trying to evaluate this latest and most unexpected development. He began carefully reviewing all he knew and all that had been said concerning Hayes Wilfred. Inevitably there came to mind his conversation with Gay Kendal relative to Wilfred. Her estimate of the man abruptly took on an interesting significance. Her opinion of Wilfred was largely based on feminine intuition, she had said; but Slade began to believe that the keen brain under her rebellious curly hair had instinctively analyzed the man from personal observation, added to what she had learned of his nature and his actions. She said that she had sensed a hardness and ruthlessnes in Hayes Wilfred that she had found disquieting. From his own observation, Slade had been inclined to agree with her, although at the time he did not attach too much significance to the probability, feeling as he did at the time that Wilfred's deformity might have developed a certain resentment against life in general because of the affliction that had been visited upon him, which translated into a certain antagonism and an overwhelming ambition to prove himself able to rise above the handicap. And when a man is fired by such an ambition he is likely to sweep all opposition aside by any means that comes to hand.

"Content is the deadly foe of ambition," Hayes Wilfred had said. Slade understood that better, now. Hayes Wilfred would never be satisfied with content, would never seek it. He preferred to live dangerously, to achieve his ambition to be preeminent among his fellows.

All of which, while an interesting character analysis and an explanation that could be advanced of the basic reasons why Hayes Wilfred might possibly indulge in questionable practices, did not bring him any nearer a solution of the problem which confronted him.

The attempt by the tramp steamer Iago di Compostella to ram and sink the little pleasure craft occupied by himself and Gay Kendal abruptly took on a new and terrible significance. Had the word gone out to drown the girl as well as El Halcon? The thought made him shiver a little. It didn't seem possible that any sane man would go to such lengths to glut his hate, but — "There is no hate like love to hatred turned!"

And gradually it dawned on Slade that if he was right in his conjecture, he was dealing with a man touched by insanity and with all the ruthless cunning of the mad. That is, if Hayes Wilfred really was the mastermind back of what had happened. Of which, as he admitted to Cock Badding, he had no proof.

And to further complicate matters, Rance Donner remained an enigma. Slade swore wearily and rolled a cigarette. He was smoking morosely when Badding returned to the office. The labor contractor glanced at him expectantly.

"Well?" he asked.

"It isn't," Slade replied. "Nothing is. I don't know what to think or what to do. I don't recall ever being so baffled by a situation."

Badding sat down and lighted a cigar. "As I recall, from what you told me," he remarked reflectively, "several times the hellions laid a trap for you."

"And only bull luck prevented them from making a finish job of it," Slade interpolated gloomily.

"Perhaps, but I'd have another name for it," Badding said. "Each time in one way or another, by your own initiative, you managed to slip out before the jaws really closed on you. I wouldn't call that luck. But what I was getting at, wonder if it wouldn't be possible to lay a trap for them? I've a notion that if you really set your head to it, you can figure something that'll work. There's an old saying, you know, 'Set a thief to catch a thief.' Here's a little theory of mine: I'd say that somebody has been trying to horn in on it. The blowing up of the Albatross the day you arrived here was a sample of it, I'd say. And I'd also say that the reason somebody is so anxious to get rid of you is because somebody figures you're here to horn in on a good thing. What do you think?"

"I think you're very probably right on all counts, and that your suggestion is a good one," Slade replied. "The only thing to figure, a rather large order, is how, when, and where to set the trap."

"Oh, you'll find a way," Badding predicted cheerfully, adding, "And I want to be right there when it's sprung."

"You'll be plenty of help," Slade agreed.

For some time Slade sat smoking and thinking, while Badding watched him in respectful silence.

"Cock," he said suddenly, "when does the Orpheus load?"

158

"Not for several days," Badding replied. "She'll give the crew shore leave and her cargo won't head this way until word is received that she's in port."

"And what will her cargo consist of, have you any idea?"

"Hides, tallow and wool," Badding answered. "That's what she always loads. Wilfred has a contract with the shippers."

"Hides, tallow and wool," Slade repeated thoughtfully. "Sounds innocent enough." Badding nodded agreement. Slade abruptly changed the subject.

"Do you happen to know just when Rance Donner began operating out of Corpus Christi?"

"Something like five years back, best I remember," Badding answered. "I recall he was here four or five months before Hayes Wilfred started here. I remember fairly accurately because I got most of Donner's account and then when Wilfred showed up I tried to get his also, but he went to Oswell. You see, after the big hurricane wiped out Indianola as a port and the currents and tides of Matagorda Bay choked up the Lavaca channel and put Port Lavaca out of business, most of the shipping from those places came to Corpus Christi and we got quite a few new owners."

"I see," Slade nodded. "Something better than five years back he started in business here."

Again Slade was silent for some minutes.

"And Hayes Wilfred arrived a few months later. Wonder if he didn't have any use for Donner right from the beginning?"

"Hard to tell," said Badding. "I know he hasn't any use for him now, but Donner never says a thing about Wilfred. You'd think he didn't know he exists for all the attention he pays to him."

"Which is interesting," Slade commented. "Enmity is usually mutual. Interesting also that two men who appear to be enemies and who set up in business here almost at the same time should be the ones to give us a prime headache."

"Drop a loop on both of 'em and you may not be too far off the course," grunted Badding. "Maybe they're working in cahoots."

"Rather improbable, I'd say," Slade smiled. "If they're both mixed up in it, much more likely they'd be rivals. But I am getting a sort of murky notion as to how the business is conducted."

"Yes?"

"Yes. Admitting for the sake of the argument and only for the sake of the argument, for nothing has been proven, that Hayes Wilfred is the moving spirit back of the transactions, the Orpheus, an eminently respectable ship, and perhaps others in her class in some way load contraband here at Corpus Christi. Then they deliver it to that obscure cove in Honduras where it is transshipped to some old tramp such as the Iago di Compostella whose possible loss would mean little. The tramp runs the cargo to some place on the Mexican coast where it is received by the consignees, supposedly the backers of what they call the revolution."

"But how do they load it here at Corpus Christi?"

"That," Slade said, "remains to be learned. By the way, where do the hides and tallow and wool that form the Orpheus' cargo come from?"

"Mostly from over west of here," Badding answered. "Lots of little sheep and goat ranches over there and they do plenty of slaughtering. The Mexicans are very fond of *cabritos*, as they call the young goats, and of mutton. The little spreads do a thriving business with them and sell the tallow, hides and wool as by-products. Late this evening the freight wagons will roll out of town and head west to make the pick-ups."

"No doubt there is some central holding spot where the loads are assembled," Slade observed reflectively.

"Sounds reasonable," Badding admitted. "I don't know much about it, though; never gave it any thought. I know the wagons take along barrels and baling wire."

Slade nodded and for some moments sat smoking and gazing out the window, the concentration furrow deep between his brows.

"Cock," he said suddenly, "I'm going to play a hunch."

"Yes? How's that?"

"I'm going to trail that wagon train tonight and see if I can get a look at what they load.'

"But, blazes! they wouldn't be loading guns and stuff they couldn't get through the Customs," Badding objected.

"I know, but if all our theorizing isn't completely off-trail, the stuff gets on the Orpheus somehow, and I feel that somehow it's connected with the stuff the wagons pick up. As I said, I'm playing a hunch, but sometimes hunches pay off."

"You've got something there," Badding conceded. "Want me to go along? As I told you, I used to be a cowhand and can ride."

"Hardly necessary, under the circumstances," Slade declined the offer. "All I have in mind is a little spying, and I can do that alone. I'm not going to get into a rukus with the wagons."

"Maybe not, but sometimes rukuses come along when you're not expecting them," Badding returned dubiously.

"Don't worry, I'll call on you when I need you," Slade promised, "but I don't figure I will this trip."

Badding still looked doubtful, but did not comment further.

Slade stood up and glanced at the westering sun. "Be seeing you," he said, and left the office.

CHAPTER
SEVENTEEN

Not knowing how long he might be gone, Slade packed staple provisions in his saddle pouches, along with his small skillet and little flat bucket. Then he rode out of town through the red-gold sunshine of late afternoon. He rode east, so that if anybody was keeping tabs on his movement, which he thought very probable, they would think he was headed for the Tumbling K ranchhouse and a visit with Clark Kendal. He rode steadily for several miles, then, making sure he wasn't wearing a tail, he left the trail and rode north, then west, bypassing Corpus Christi in a wide circle. Four or five miles beyond the town he veered south until he could sight the trail. Locating a convenient thicket, from which he could see without being seen, he holed up and waited.

It was quite a long wait, for almost full dark had fallen before the wagon train put in an appearance. Accompanying it were four mounted men, which Slade thought rather unusual. Wagons in quest of hides and tallow were not often convoyed by outriders.

Slade watched the big wains, four of them, crawl past and grow indistinct in the deepening gloom. He followed at a discreet distance, with the train barely visible in the starlight.

Mile after mile he rode; he estimated he had covered at least twenty when the shadowy train turned from the main trail to follow a narrower and much less travelled track that wound north. Reaching the intersection without incident, Slade followed, drawing closer, for there was a good deal of chaparral lining the trail, the visibility was bad, and for the moment he could not see the wagons. Eventually, however, he sighted them again and held his distance. Another seven or eight miles flowed past under Shadow's hoofs and to the right, set back some distance from the trail, appeared a group of buildings. There was a barn, what looked to be a bunkhouse, and an old ranchhouse with lighted windows. The wagons turned into the yard and came to a halt. Slade approached as near as he dared and reined Shadow in against the bristle of growth. He felt sure he could not be seen from where the wagons stood but had a pretty good view of what went on.

Plenty was going on and without delay. As Slade watched, a big fire was lighted, the barrels were unloaded from the wagons and placed nearby. Two huge kettles were hung over the blaze. Evidently the tallow was to be melted down and then poured into the barrels, the customary procedure.

The front door of the ranchhouse had opened when the wagons arrived. Men began coming out carrying something, just what Slade could not at that distance ascertain. They grouped around the barrels and were very busy at something. Again the watching Ranger could not see with what they were occupying themselves.

"Feller, for all the good I'm doing, we might as well not be here," he whispered to the horse. "I've got to get a look at what's going on around that fire."

With which he turned Shadow's head and rode slowly back down the trail, hoping that the dust would muffle his hoofbeats enough to make them inaudible to the men gathered at the fire. Where the growth was a little thinner he pushed the black into it and dropped the split reins to the ground.

"Stay put," he told him. "I'll be seeing you, I hope."

Keeping close to the growth, where the shadow was deepest, he stole back toward the ranchhouse. With the fire in sight, he paused and studied the lay of the land. After a careful inspection, he believed he should be able to circle around to the back of the ranchhouse, slide along its side wall and get a good view of the mysterious activities around the fire.

Careful to break no twig, to step on no dry branch or loose stone, he wormed his way through the growth until he was opposite the back of the house. All was dark. There was no sound from that direction, no hint of motion. Taking a deep breath, he slipped across the starlit open space to reach the sanctuary of the wall, inched along it to almost the far corner and paused. Less than a score of yards distant was the fire over which swung the kettles.

Men were packing something into the barrels; Slade's eye caught a gleam of metal. Two more, wielding big ladles, were scooping the melted tallow from the kettles and pouring it into other barrels. It took a surprisingly few helpings from the ladles to fill the barrels. Hammer blows sounded as heads were nailed in place.

The men laughed and talked as they worked; one was singing a ribald song. Evidently they had no fear of interruption. Slade strained to get a good look at their faces, but at that distance they were mere whitish blurs in the play of light and shadow cast by the flickering fire.

So engrossed was he in the scene before him that he paid no heed to his immediate suroundings. He whirled at a sound behind him. A man loomed in the gloom.

"What you doin' here, Cully," he growled. "You oughta — hey! You ain't Cully!"

Slade's lunging hand stifled the yell rising in his throat, and instantly he was fighting for his life. The fellow was almost as tall as himself and heavier. He went for his gun, but Slade pinned his hand against his thigh before he could grip the butt. His free hand belabored the Ranger with heavy blows. Slade snugged his face against the other's breast and held on, striving to throttle his opponent before he was himself beaten into insensibility. Madly they reeled back and forth, bumping against the wall of the house, lurching, staggering. Had the bunch around the fire not been making such a racket, they would have assuredly heard the sounds of the struggle.

A loose stone slipped under Slade's foot, throwing him off balance for an instant. The fellow tore free with a strangled yell of triumph. Even as his gun leaped from the holster, Slade hit him square and true on the angle of the jaw. The gun blazed as he fell and the bullet whistled past Slade's ear. It blazed again as Slade streaked it for the growth. The slug hit the heel of his boot and nearly knocked him off his feet. From the fire sounded yells of alarm. Then a fusillade of shots that buzzed around the fleeing Ranger like angry hornets and showered him with twigs as he dived into the chaparral. Heedless of thorns, he tore through it to where Shadow waited and flung himself into the saddle. Behind was a wild uproar that bellowed through the silence of the night. He settled himself in the hull and rode at top speed for the main trail and Corpus Christi, seething with anger directed at himself. What had looked for a moment like an open-and-shut case had gone a-glimmering, and because of his own infernal carelessness!

"Appears I've developed a positive genius of late for doing the wrong things," he wrathfully told the horse. Shadow snorted cheerful agreement and stretched his legs.

It was full daylight when Slade reached Corpus Christi. He stabled Shadow and repaired to Cock Badding's office. Unlocking it, he sat down, rolled a cigarette and waited for the labor contractor to put in an appearance.

Badding stared in astonishment when he entered the office, an hour or so later.

"What the devil happened?" he demanded. "Your face is all scratched and swollen!"

Slade told him. Badding swore explosively. "So that's the way they do it!" he sputtered.

167

"Yes, that's one of the ways they do it," Slade corrected. "A simple and clever method. Fill the barrels with rifle parts, pour in enough melted tallow to conceal them after it congeals. The cargo shipped by an owner with Hayes Wilfred's excellent reputation would undergo only a cursory inspection by the Customs people; they wouldn't prod into the tallow. Everything was going nicely till I muddled it by not paying attention to what was going on around me."

"Chances are they figured it was just some wandering cowpoke and didn't pay it much mind." Badding strove to comfort him. "All you've got to do is sit tight and grab 'em when they roll in with those barrels."

"Wait and see," Slade predicted grimly.

Rising to his feet, he pinched out his cigarette. "If you don't mind, I'm going to clean up a bit and go to bed," he announced. "I don't feel so chipper."

"Go to it, get a good rest," said Badding. "You'll feel better when you wake up."

On his way to bed, Slade paused at the telegraph office to see if there might be a message from Captain McNelty.

There was. He read it and whistled under his breath. "No wonder I keep thinking those jiggers reminded me of somebody else," he muttered. "Well, if this doesn't take the hide off the barn door!"

Tired and sleepy though he was, he headed right back to Badding's office and handed him the telegram. Badding's eyes almost popped from his head as he read —

"More concerning J. W. Donner. Estate largely ships. Left to his two sons Rance H. and Hayes Wilfred Donner."

"Brothers!" gurgled Badding. "The two hellions are brothers!"

"Yes," Slade nodded. "All the time when I looked at one of them I kept feeling that I'd recently seen somebody who looked a lot like him. No wonder!"

"Now I know they're in cahoots!" declared Badding. "Can't you grab that blasted dwarf for going around under an assumed name?"

"No law that I know of which says a man can't use only part of his name if he's of a mind to," Slade replied. "Could say he didn't want to go into competition with his brother under the name of Donner. Or that he had a falling out with his family and broke with them to the extent of renouncing the family name. Or any one of a number of legitimate reasons. I'm going to bed."

"And I think I'm going out and get drunk, blankety-blank-blank- it!" swore Badding.

Two days later the wagon train rolled up to the piers, heaped high with bundles of hides and bales of wool. There was not a tallow barrel in sight!

"See?" Slade said to Badding.

The next evening, the Orpheus spread her white wings and sailed gaily out of Corpus Christi harbor.

Cock Badding shook his fist at the departing vessel. "If ships could laugh, I'd swear that blasted thing is laughing at us," he growled.

"Perhaps," Slade smiled, adding, "But I don't think its owner is exactly chortling under his whiskers. Having his neat little scheme uncovered and his valuable shipment delayed doesn't set too well with him, I imagine. The chances are he's just about as put out as we are and with more reason. The shadow of possible consequences always hangs over him. He may not sleep too well of nights. 'The guilty flee when no man pursueth.'"

Badding suddenly had an idea. "By the way, how about those barrels of rifles?" he asked. "Suppose you could tie onto them, wouldn't that help?"

Slade shook his head. "Again, no case," he replied. "Nothing in the law that says you can't pack rifle parts in tallow. Intended to be smuggled into Mexico to be used against a friendly government? Prove it! Even the Customs people couldn't do anything about it. Besides, the chances are they were moved away from there in a hurry and hidden some place. That ranchhouse, I think, is an old deserted property used by the bunch as a sort of headquarters and gathering place. They're not likely to use it again."

Badding gave a groan of despair. "Looks like there's no way to drop a loop on the hellions," he lamented.

"There'll be a way," Slade predicted confidently. "Sooner or later they'll make a slip; they always do."

"I hope so, but it sure don't look too good," Badding said morosely. "Well, it's quitting time. I'm going home and take it easy. I'm scared this business is getting me down; I'm wasting away to a shadow."

170

Looking at his brawny form, Slade felt that he was a decidedly substantial shadow.

"See you in the morning," he said and headed for the Kinney House and something to eat.

Slade enjoyed a leisurely dinner and then sat for some time smoking and thinking; he had plenty to think on. The strangest and most perplexing angle of the whole affair, he felt, was the revelation that Hayes Wilfred and Rance Donner were brothers. Now he realized how marked was the resemblance. Rance Donner's hair had more red in it, his features were somewhat more roughly hewn, but they were strikingly similar in line and contour to Wilfred's, and so was the expression, the coloring and shape of the eyes. Both had the big shoulders, deep chest and long arms. Below the waist lay the great difference. Wilfred's grotesquely short, bowed but powerful legs were in shocking contrast to Rance Donner's long, straight and graceful limbs. Slade wondered if Wilfred had not secretly envied his tall, finely formed and ruggedly handsome brother.

Yes, it was not improbable. And maybe the envy had gradually crystallized into hate. Clark Kendal said that Wilfred had no use for Rance Donner, and the momentary flash of his eyes when they rested on his brother standing at the bar of the Kinney House confirmed Kendal's subsequent remark.

Slade wondered if the hatred was reciprocated by Rance Donner. Upon due reflection, he decided that he did not think so. He felt, in fact, with nothing concrete on which to base the feeling, that Rance Donner was

171

not capable of hating anyone. Truculent, salty, ready to fight at the drop of a hat, he nevertheless was, Slade believed, the kind of an individual who would knock a man down and then help him to his feet and have a drink with him.

Indeed, Slade was of the opinion that Ranch Donner and Cock Badding were cast in much the same mold. He could vision them having a rukus over something, jeering and grinning at each other while they hammered away until one or both was exhausted and then sitting down in all good fellowship to review, with laughter and chuckles, salient points of the battle.

And then going at it again, hammer and tongs, when something else came up over which they could not agree.

He chuckled himself and strolled to the bar for a drink. After emptying his glass he left the hotel and sauntered along busy Leopard Street. The sun was just going down and it was a beautiful evening. Slade abruptly turned around and walked the other way. To the devil with it all! Forget the whole blasted business for a while. He headed for Shadow's stable, got the rig on the big black and rode east at a fast pace.

Arriving at the Tumbling K ranchhouse without mishap, he was hilariously greeted by the hands loafing about. One relieved him of Shadow and he mounted the veranda steps and walked into the living room, the door of which stood hospitably open. And seated in an arm chair and appearing very much at ease, was the man who had been occupying his thoughts.

172

Hayes Wilfred — Hayes Wilfred Donner, rather — waved a cordial hand, but Slade thought there was a derisive gleam in his clear, pale eyes.

"How are you, Mr. Slade?" he greeted the Ranger. "As I said during our previous conversation, once a cowhand always a cowhand. You're not content unless you're taking long rides."

Slade wondered if there was a hidden meaning in the apparently innocent remark. Recently he *had* taken quite a long ride. A ride that had proven far from satisfactory. Perhaps Wilfred was amusedly referring to that. Subtly poking fun at the man he quite likely regarded as his adversary seeking to horn in on the off-color but lucrative business in which he was engaged. El Halcon! horning in to skim off the cream!

Let him have his fun. Before all was finished, he might laugh on the other side of his face, as the saying went.

"You appear to be fond of riding yourself, Mr. Wilfred," he answered smilingly.

"Oh, I drop in on Clark every now and then," Wilfred replied. "He and I are old *amigos* and we have business dealings. He'll show up shortly — out riding with Miss Gay."

Kendal and his daughter did arrive before long; both looked surprised and pleased.

"Well, well, this is fine!" boomed old Clark. "Come along, time to eat. Slade, that feller Peterby is a real find; I think I've put on ten pounds since he started rustlin' the pots and pans. And look at Gay!"

"I am, but I don't see any difference," Slade smiled.

After a snack and a short session in the office with Kendal, Hayes Wilfred departed.

"A lot to do," he explained. "Another ship due in tomorrow and I want to be present at the loading. Besides," he added, "like Mr. Slade, I enjoy riding under the stars."

His eyes rested fleetingly on Gay's face as he spoke, their expression, Slade thought, startlingly similar to that they wore when they regarded Rance Donner's entrance at the Kinney House bar. Slade was beginning to think Gay had been right: Wilfred hated her.

Kendal said goodnight and walked to the door with his guest. Then he turned to Slade.

"You aren't trailing your twine tonight, I hope," he said. "Stick around."

"But I'll have to leave early in the morning," Slade qualified his acceptance. "Don't want to be late for work."

"I'll see to it that you are awake in time," Gay said, her eyes dancing.

"But are you sure you'll be awake?" Slade asked pointedly.

"Oh, I've got a very reliable alarm clock now," she replied. "We have a new rooster in the chicken yard who starts yelling promptly at daybreak. He has a crow like a locomotive whistle and uses it."

"He'll end up getting his neck wrung, if he don't tighten the latigo on his beak," old Clark predicted darkly. "I threw a shoe at him this morning. Missed him."

174

The rooster saw to it that Slade was awake at daybreak; never before had he heard a fowl kick up such a racket. The rest of the house was not yet astir, but Gay insisted on getting his breakfast before he rode to town.

"I wouldn't think of you leaving hungry," she declared. "And I'll even help you get the rig on your horse."

"You're spoiling me completely," he complained. "Don't see how I'll ever make out without you."

"Oh, you'll get along," she said lightly, but her eyes were a trifle wistful.

Slade felt much better for the night at the Tumbling K ranchhouse. His mind was clear and the problems that had seemed crushing the day before were viewed from a more optimistic perspective. He sang softly to himself in his rich sweet voice as Shadow's hoofs clicked merrily on the trail and marvelled at the Autumnal beauty of the range. The waves of the rolling land resembled those of the swelling sea frozen while in motion and gleamed golden in the rays of the rising sun. The grass heads were tipped with amethyst and a little breeze shook down dewgems from every branch and twig. Birds sang in the thickets, rejoicing in the newborn day, and little animals went about their small businesses in a perky manner. It was good to be alive, Slade thought, even though he was beset by a vexatious riddle that seemed to defy his ingenuity. Well, he'd read riddles aright before, and doubtless would this one.

He reviewed recent happenings, endeavoring to properly evaluate their significance and to neglect no overlooked detail. Gradually he arrived at the conclusion that Cock Badding might have been wiser than appeared at first glance when he suggested it might be a good notion to try and locate the tallow barrels filled with rifle parts. Wilfred would doubtless endeavor to slip the valuable cargo out of the country and to its destination in one way or another. What that way would be, Slade at the moment had no idea. Certainly not by way of one of his ships dropping anchor at Corpus Christi. But if the barrels were located they might well lead him to the solution of the problem. Before he reached Corpus Christi he had resolved on a course of action.

"I aim to take a little ride tonight and may come in late tomorrow," he told Badding that evening at quitting time.

"Go to it and come in whenever you're of a mind to," said Badding. "Hit on something?"

"If so, I have you to thank," Slade replied. "Tell you about it later."

It was nearing midnight when Slade left the Kinney House by way of a side door and walked swiftly to Shadow's stable. Before entering, he stood for some time in the gloom against the wall to make sure nobody was keeping a watch on his movements. Reassured by the lack of sound or motion, he got the rig on the big black and rode west at a swift pace. On the first hilltop he drew rein and surveyed the back trail for several minutes. It lay deserted in the starlight. He rode on, estimating that he should reach the side track on which

176

the old ranchhouse stood in the dark hour that preceded the dawn.

"We're just playing a hunch, feller, but the last time we were out here we were playing a hunch that would have paid off except for my stupidity," he told Shadow. "This time maybe I can keep from falling over my own feet."

Shadow's answering snort indicated that he was plainly unconvinced. Slade chuckled and rode on.

When he reached the side track he slowed to a walk, peering and listening. A hundred yards or so below where the building stood, he gently forced Shadow into the growth and dropped the split reins to the ground.

"Be seeing you soon," he whispered and crept on through the tangle of chaparral until he reached a spot from which he could obtain a view of the house, which stood dark and lonely and ominous looking in the faint sheen of starlight seeping through an overcast of gauzy cloud. He could see that the front door was closed. The windows had the appearance of staring eyes, with no gleam of light behind them. The door of the nearby bunkhouse sagged on its hinges. The barn door was like to the yawning mouth of a monster waiting to engulf its prey. All in all, an eerie setting not calculated to soothe the nerves and fill one with a sense of well being.

In fact, it had just the opposite effect on Slade. He experienced a feeling of disquietude, of apprehension. The ancient building seemed to exude a nameless threat, as if some effluvium of past horrors gathered about it. And a warning voice dinned soundlessly on his ears —

177

"Go away! Go away! Here is an evil place, a place of sin, and horror, and blood — go away! go away!"

He cursed his vivid imagination that built up these formless terrors in his mind, but even the monotonous chirping of a cricket in a nearby bush translated to the words, "Go — back! Go — back!" Slade realized that his palms were sweating, that there was a film of moisture on his upper lip, although the night was cool. With difficulty he got a grip on himself and awaited the dawn.

It came slowly, gray in the east, then a flush of primrose. What had been blurred clumps of shadow took on sharp edges, a distinctness of line and form. The old house looked a little better in the strengthening light, but not much. Silent, apparently deserted it stood, shrinking away from the glory of the morning, huddling back toward the gloom of the night. No trickle of smoke arose from its chimney. No gleam of brightness showed back of the staring eyes that were its windows. No sound broke its unearthly silence.

If anybody was in there, now was the time they would be stirring, the Ranger reasoned. He'd wait a little while longer before risking an approach to the sinister building. Leaning against a tree trunk, confident that he could not be spotted in the thick growth, he continued to search the nearby terrain for any sign of life.

Birds were singing. A couple of little rodents whisked across the clearing, approached the closed door without fear, nibbled around the sill and departed with no indication of alarm. Slade waited a little longer, then took a step forward. And now the chirp of the cricket seemed to say, "Come — back! Come — back!"

"To the devil with you, rattle-brain!" he muttered and walked briskly to the closed door, poised for instant action. He reached it without incident, paused to listen. The house remained silent as the tomb. He reached a hand for the door knob, then halted, his fingers barely touching the rounded surface.

In men who ride much alone with danger as a constant stirrup companion, there develops a subtle sixth sense that warns of peril when none, apparently, exists. And now this voiceless monitor was setting up a clamor in his brain. Slade always catalogued it as the result of something that automatically registered on his keen senses but not audibly. He had learned not to disregard that seemingly senseless premonition. Standing motionless, he studied the door. Perhaps somebody *was* in there, waiting. Somebody who had noticed his approach and was now just waiting for him to open the door and stand outlined against the glare of the sunshine. He still could hear no sound, but as his fingers tightened on the knob, the clamor in his brain rose to a strident though soundless shriek. He eased back beyond the door. Standing where the hinges clamped against the building wall, he could still reach the knob. By imperceptible degrees he turned it until he knew that the bolt was all the way back in its socket; then with a quick jerk, he flung the door wide open.

There was a crashing roar. Buckshot howled through the opening, so close that Slade felt the lethal breath of

179

its passing. He went back along the wall a half dozen steps and crouched, a gun in each hand.

Nothing more happened; there was no further sound inside the building. For long moments he crouched motionless, then edged forward again, listening, peering. He uttered a hollow groan, simulating the agonized plaint of a badly wounded man; and still nothing happened. Smoke rings drifted lazily out the door, and that was all. Balancing his hat on one gun barrel, he thrust it forward past the door jamb, without results. Deciding to take a chance, he glided ahead until he could see through the opening — and looked squarely into the yawning twin muzzles of a sawed-off shotgun!

CHAPTER
EIGHTEEN

Slade was back along the wall almost to the far corner before the truth of what he saw really registered. He growled an oath and strode back to the door, pausing to stare at the infernal contraption which had been rigged up, for his especial benefit, he felt sure. The cunning hellion had surmised that there was a good chance of him coming snooping around and had prepared a "reception committee" for him.

Clamped rigidly to an upright nailed to the floor was the shotgun, its triggers wired by a line which extended to the inner door knob, so that anyone opening the door and starting in would get the double charge of buckshot dead center.

With a glance at the stairway leading to an upper story, Slade walked through a second room to the rear of the house. Trained on the back door was a shotgun similarly rigged, the hammers at full cock. He carefully lowered the hammers. Some chance wanderer might try to enter that way and get blown from under his hat.

The shotgun trap was all. There were no furnishings in the house and investigation showed no signs of the tallow barrels crammed with rifle parts, upstairs or down, only the big kettles in which the tallow was melted. Slade rolled a cigarette, leaned against the wall and smoked thoughtfully. Belatedly he recalled that the shotgun blast would have been heard for a considerable distance. He stepped out the door, glancing around, and at that instant a man rode into the clearing from the north. He jerked his mount to a halt. Slade saw his hand flash down and went for his guns.

Back and forth gushed the flickers of flame and the spurts of smoke. Slade heard the whine of passing lead, close, and fired with both hands. The horseman rose in his saddle; the gun dropped from his hand. For a moment he poised rigid, then toppled slowly sideways like a falling tree to hit the ground with a thud. The horse plunged forward a few steps, halted and gazed back inquiringly at the still form.

Slade approached the body warily, but the fellow was satisfactorily dead, two bullets laced through his heart. He was a big man and his hardlined face had a slightly familiar look; Slade couldn't be sure, but he believed he was the man with whom he had the wring the night he was surprised watching the rifle parts stowed in the tallow barrels.

"And I came darn near tangling my twine again," he growled. "If he'd slipped up and caught me in the house, very likely right now we'd be occupying reverse positions. I appear to be getting no better fast."

Squatting down, he carefully went through the dead man's pockets, which disgorged a rather large sum of money, the various odds and ends usually carried by range riders, and a scrap of paper on which was written in a very legible hand —

With wrinkled brows, Slade puzzled over the cryptic notation. The figures, he concluded, very likely signified a date; he pondered a moment. This was Tuesday, the 15th of October, the tenth month. Yes, that was probably it. Friday would be the 18th. Looked like perhaps there was a meeting of some sort in the city of the Alamo, which the fellow was instructed to attend. What that could mean, Slade hadn't the slightest notion. He certainly wouldn't have had much time to get there by the 18th. Pocketing the paper, he dismissed it for the time being. Straightening up, he rolled a cigarette and smoked slowly, eyeing the trail that wound northward. Where had the hellion come from? Presumably from no great distance, if the sound of the shotgun blast had drawn him to the vicinity. Slade became very curious as to that and resolved to try and find out. He dismissed the notion of retrieving Shadow and riding the trail. The fellow might possibly have had companions who would likely come to investigate the shooting, were they within hearing distance. He'd be better off on foot, presuming wherever the fellow came from was not far away. His ears strained to catch the sound of approaching hoofbeats, he stole up the track, keeping close to the encroaching growth. Very quickly he concluded that wagons had passed that way no great time before. Which was interesting.

He had proceeded something more than half a mile when he halted and sniffed sharply; to his nostrils had come the unmistakeable tang of wood smoke. For minutes he stood motionless, pressed against the growth, poised to dive into it; but still there was no sound ahead. With even greater caution he moved on. The trail curved slightly and emptied into a clearing where sat a big old cabin roughly but tightly built. Near the cabin was a leanto which would accommodate a dozen horses or more. At present there were no horses under it, however, which Slade took to be a good sign. A little farther on were several big wagons.

Again the Ranger stood motionless, peering and listening. Reassured by the continued lack of sound, he risked issuing from his place of concealment against the brush and advanced to the cabin, every nerve strung for instant action. Above the chimney top, he noted, was a bluish haze, the faint smoke of a dying fire. The door stood open and when he reached it he peered in.

There was no sign of human occupancy at the moment, although plenty of signs that the condition had not prevailed in the immediate past. On a rusty iron stove a coffee pot steamed slightly, a pot of beans simmered. There were bunks built along two of the walls, a table and chairs, shelves upon which rested a store of provisions. In a corner stood several score rifles. And stacked in three tiers, occupying half the room, were the tallow barrels which doubtlessly contained rifle parts. He had found the real headquarters of the smuggling gang.

Yes, this was it. Doubtless the cabin was always occupied by some member of the outfit posing as a prospector or hunter. Here was where the contraband was kept, under guard. The old ranchhouse was in the nature of a base of operations, where the tallow was melted, the rifle parts fitted into the barrels. The trail showed evidence of practically no usage for many years. A very clever set-up.

But now that he had found it, what the devil was he going to do with it? Still nothing on which he could base an effective court action. Well, he'd think of something.

The coffee looked inviting. He filled a tin cup from the steaming pot and drank it slowly. Then he added a little water to the beans so that they would not crisp on the dying fire. When somebody showed up, it would look like the cabin guard had just ridden off somewhere. The small quantity of beans in the pot seemed to indicate that he had not anticipated company in the near future and had been preparing a meal for only his own consumption. Slade felt that he was reasonably safe from interruption for a while. Mustn't play his luck too strong, however.

With this in mind he closed the door and hurried back to the ranchhouse. All was as he left it. Without delay he got busy, carrying the body into the growth and heaping brush over it and the saddle which he removed from the horse that was contentedly cropping grass. Some distance down the main trail he would turn the animal loose to fend for itself, which it could easily do until somebody picked it up. He closed the front door of the ranchhouse, feeling confident that when the smugglers returned, seeing the doors apparently untampered with, they would conclude that nobody had been around during their absence and would not be likely to enter the house by way of a window to further investigate. Looping the bridle ever his arm, he led the smuggler's horse to where he had left Shadow, mounted and headed for the main trail, which, when he reached it, lay deserted in both directions. After covering a few miles, he removed the bridle from the led horse, tossed it into the brush, and left the animal to its own devices.

All the while he was puzzling over the cryptic notation on the slip of paper taken from the dead man's pocket. What the devil could the supposed meeting in San Antonio portend? San Antonio was a long ways from Corpus Christi Bay.

Abruptly he straightened in the saddle, his eyes glowing. Corpus Christi Bay! The bay!

"Horse," he exclaimed, "I believe I've got it! That note doesn't refer to the city of San Antonio, but to San Antonio Bay, thirty-some miles east of Corpus Christi. Ships can enter that bay and cross it to the mouth of the San Antonio River, which merges with the Guadalupe a few miles to the northwest of the bay. She'll slip in under cover of darkness Friday night and the stuff will be there waiting for her to load. Yes, I'll bet a hatful of pesos that is it. Horse, business is going to pick up!"

He circled Corpus Christi and entered the town from the east, against the possibility of prying eyes. After stabling Shadow, his first stop was the sheriff's office. In detail, he told Sheriff Cole of what had happened and what he had dicovered.

186

"By gosh! it looks like you've hit the jackpot," exclaimed Cole. "Yes, I believe you've figured it right. Just how do you aim to handle it?"

"We'll get a posse together, slip 'em out of town one or two at a time and head for San Antonio Bay where the river empties into it," Slade said. "That'll be the logical place for the ship to put in. When she loads the stuff, we'll have our excuse to grab her."

"And put a smuggling charge against the hellions, eh?"

"If things work out as I expect them to, we'll be able to lodge a charge of murder against them," Slade said grimly. "Remember, nine men, including the captain, died when the Albatross was blown up. And two more who must have had some knowledge of how it was done were murdered to shut their mouths."

"Wonder who that ship belonged to," remarked the sheriff.

"I gathered from Badding that the captain was the owner," Slade replied. "In my opinion he was trying to horn in on the arms running business and was eliminated and his ship destroyed. Very likely he was packing a lot of powder — it was a powder explosion, not dynamite, that destroyed the ship."

"Chances are you're right," agreed Cole. "How many men should we take with us? I have four deputies."

"Badding will want to go and he's a good man and can ride; that'll make seven," Slade counted. "I'd say three or four specials, if you can round up that many who know how to keep a tight latigo on their jaws, should be enough."

"I'll get 'em," promised the sheriff. "Yep, that ought to do the trick, with the element of surprise in our favor."

"But the greatest care must be taken to keep the move secret, otherwise *we* may get a surprise we won't like," Slade warned. "Well, I'm going to get something to eat and then have a talk with Badding. See you later tonight, if you'll be in the office."

"I'll be here," the sheriff answered. "Meanwhile I'll have a talk with the boys and line them up. What about a meeting place?"

Slade considered a moment. "I think I'll ride out to the Tumbling K tomorow and have a little talk with Clark Kendal," he said. "His ranchhouse would do fine, and I feel pretty sure he'll go along with us."

"He'll go along with us all right, and he'll want to be in at the finish," the sheriff predicted confidently. "That old hellion never misses a fight if there's a chance to horn in. Only," he added doubtfully, "he's pretty close friends with Wilfred."

"Not so close but that he'll be able to recognize the truth when it's placed before him," Slade replied. "And when he is made to see that it was Wilfred's infernal schemes that nearly cost his daughter's life, I've a notion he won't feel very kindly toward *Senor* Wilfred."

"Yes, I guess that's so," Cole agreed. "By the way, there's just one catch to this business. Where we're headed for is outside Neuces County, where I have no authority."

"I've thought of that," Slade replied. "I'll swear you all in as a Ranger's posse. Will mean revealing my

Ranger connections, but there's no help for it. I don't want a single loophole through which the cunning devil might wriggle."

"That should take care of everything," Cole nodded. "Be seeing you."

Cock Badding was elated at the prospect of a brush with the outlaws. "Haven't had a good wring for a coon's age," he chortled. "You think there'll be a real ruckus?"

"I doubt if they'll surrender without one," Slade replied. "They're desperate men, with always the shadow of the noose hanging over them. Yes, I think that very likely there'll be a fight; we'll be mighty lucky to get by without one."

"Who wants to be that lucky?" Badding said cheerfully. "I'll oil up my shootin' iron tonight, and I ain't exactly a snide with one. If I shoot at a jigger and he don't fall, I go around behind him to see what's holding him up."

Slade did ride to the Tumbling K ranchhouse the following evening. With the door locked and the shades drawn, he produced the star of the Rangers, to the vast astonishment of old Clark.

Gay, however, did not appear particularly surprised. "We should have known it. You do things like I've always heard the Rangers do, and you're just like what I've always imagined a Ranger would be like."

"Some of them are smarter and always get their man, easily," Slade laughingly replied.

"*Man?*" said Gay, lifting her brows and smiling.

As Slade outlined, step by step, his case against Hayes Wilfred, Kendal's initial amazement and disbelief changed to furious anger.

"The ornery hyderphobia skunk!" he stormed. "Just wait till I get a chance to line sights with the sidewinder! I've a notion to ride to town in the morning and shoot it out with him."

"No, you won't," Slade contradicted him. "Taking the law in your own hands is bad business, as a number of sheriffs and marshals have told El Halcon."

"The terrapin-brains!" growled Kendal. "Nobody that's known you for an hour would put any stock in that El Halcon sheep dip. And the boys want to hole up here? Fine! Send 'em along. And when you ride to drop a loop on those wind spiders, I'm riding with you."

"And I'm taking a chance of losing both of you," Gay protested.

"Don't worry your head about us," her father replied. "We'll make out. It's those horned toads who'll need somebody to worry about them. High time this section was cleaned out. I've always said it would take the Rangers to do it. Fact is, I wrote Captain McNelty to that effect."

"He received your letter," Slade said.

"And sent you along, eh? Well, he couldn't have done better. The spavined old coot's got more brains than I give him credit for. Oh, sure I know him. Known him for forty years. When he was just a cowpoke managing somehow to keep out of jail. Reckon he figured getting into the law officer business was the only way he could do it. Let's see, this is Wednesday. Your bunch will be drifting in Friday evening, eh? We'll be ready for them and I'll see to it there are no slips. You'll be riding back to town in the morning?"

"Yes," Slade answered. "I want to be seen around the waterfront tomorrow and Friday, against the chance somebody may be keeping tabs on me. I'd like to leave early tomorrow morning."

"We still have the rooster, and he still crows," Gay observed demurely.

The following morning, before repairing to the waterfront, Slade visited the sheriff.

"All set to go," Cole told him. "Incidentally, I've had a man keeping watch on the trail for those wagons."

"Not a bad idea, but I don't think they'll use the eastwest trail," Slade said. "Very likely there is another route farther north by way of which they can reach the bay. Lots of obscure trails through the brush country for those who know them, formerly old Indian tracks."

Friday evening, as dusk was falling, Walt Slade rode east at top speed. And behind him, unseen in the deepening gloom, rode another horseman whose face was lined and haggard, but those eyes glowed with unswerving purpose.

CHAPTER
NINETEEN

Ten minutes after Slade reached the Tumbling K ranchhouse, the posse headed for San Antonio Bay, and in their wake drifted the lone horseman.

Slade rode in the van, with Sheriff Cole, Kendal and Cock Badding beside him. His face was stern and set and on his broad breast gleamed the star of the Rangers. Many a curious glance was cast at his tall form by the following possemen. El Halcon a Texas Ranger! If that don't take the rag off the bush!

Before reaching the point where the Guadalupe and San Antonio Rivers poured their combined flood into the bay, Slade veered north.

"We'll have to circle through the brush and reach the bay from the north," he explained. "Be spotted sure if we continue on the trail. The last leg we'll have to do on foot. Sounds carry a long ways on a still night like this and if we go clattering over the stones on horseback they'll be almost certain to hear us."

For nearly a mile they followed a worm-crawl course through the brush before Slade turned east again. Shortly afterward they reached a trail running from the north with a slight easterly veering, a trail that showed indications of long non-use.

"Here's their route to the bay, you can wager on that," Slade said. "Wait a minute."

He dismounted and got down on his hands and knees, peering at the surface of the track, dimly seen in the starlight.

"Yes," he said, straightening up and swinging into the saddle. "Wagon tracks, made recently. They're down there, all right. We should see the river before long. We'll slide along parallel to it until we spot something."

Another ten minutes of slow riding and they could hear the murmur of moving water. Slade called a halt.

"Leave the horses here, with one man to guard them," he directed. "It's shanks' mare for the rest of us from now on. And for Pete's sake, don't make a noise. If they hear us coming we'll get a reception we won't enjoy."

At a pace at which a respectable snail would have left them standing, the posse crept forward, pausing often to peer and listen. Once Slade turned quickly, thinking he had heard a twig snap softly somewhere in their rear; but the sound was not repeated and he saw no indication of movement in the brush behind and concluded that he had been mistaken.

Gradually a sound rose above the murmur of the river, the sounds of voices, and a bumping and scraping. Light gleamed through the foliage. Slade slowed the pace even more. Reaching a final loose fringe of chaparral, he gently parted the branches and peered out.

Before him lay the bay and a scene of bustling activity, lighted by flares and lanterns.

A battered old steamer rested against the high bank, a score or so yards distant, rising and falling on the gentle swell. A trickle of smoke rose from her rusty funnel.

"The Iago di Compostella!" Slade breathed to Badding, who nodded.

A gangplank had been lowered and men were rolling barrels up its slant to the deck, where a winch lowered them into the open main hatch. Nearby stood several big wagons, from which the barrels were unloaded. Altogether, there were nearly a dozen hardcase individuals working on the cargo or loitering around the foot of the gangplank.

"Shall we hit 'em?" whispered the sheriff, fidgeting with impatience.

"Not yet," Slade whispered back. "Wait till they're bunched. Chances are they'll go aboard for a drink or something before she shoves off. If they do, wait until they reach the deck; then we'll rush them. We should be able to reach the gangplank before they spot us."

Finally the last barrel was trundled up the gangplank, and as Slade predicted, the entire company trooped after it.

"All right," he whispered. "I'll have to give them a chance to surrender, but if they make a move, let them have it. Shoot straight and keep on shooting. Now!"

The posse streamed from concealment and rushed forward. They had almost reached the foot of the gangplank before a startled shout arose from the deck. Slade's voice rolled in thunder across the water —

"In the name of the State of Texas! You are under arrest! Elevate, you're covered!"

For an instant there was a stunned silence. Then a torrent of curses sounded from the dark group on the deck. A gun flickered and a man behind Slade yelped as the bullet found a mark.

The guns of the posse let go in a withering fire. Howls of pain echoed the reports, and a blaze of answering shots.

Weaving and ducking, shooting with both hands, Slade raced up the gangplank against the chance of the steamer roaring away from the shore and escaping. He was half way across the deck littered with bodies when a grotesque figure darted from the shadows and rushed him. The hammers of the Ranger's Colts clicked on empty shells.

Foaming, raving, Hayes Wilfred closed with him. Hands like iron vises gripped his throat. Never had Slade encountered such frightful strength. He dropped his empty guns and strove to tear loose the throttling fingers, to no avail. His companions did not dare fire at Wilfred for fear of hitting him. Slade could not breathe, his heart pounded, his laboring lungs threatened to burst his chest. The madman's contorted face and glaring eyes were close to him, enormously magnified through the mist of death crawling past his eyes. He fought with the last remnants of his failing strength, loosened the dwarf's grip a little.

Suddenly Wilfred hurled him back, floundering, reeling, off balance. With a screech of triumph he whipped a gun from a shoulder holster.

"No, Wilfred! no!" cried a voice. A tall form leaped forward, seized the dwarf's gunhand and flung it up even as Wilfred pulled trigger. The bullet whined over Slade's head. Rance Donner, for it was he, strove to keep his hold on Wilfred's wrist, but the great muscles swelled like those of a constricting snake and tore free. Wilfred leaped back, lining the gun with his brother's breast.

Back too far! With an awful shriek he vanished down the black yawn of the open main hatch. The thud of his broken body shivered up from the dark depths.

With Wilfred's death, all resistance ceased. The sailors, who had taken no part in the fight, were lined along the rail, their hands raised. Beside them, hands also high in the air, stood five sullen outlaws. The others had preceded their leader to open the gates of Hades to receive him.

Automatically, Slade picked up his fallen guns and holstered them; he turned to Rance Donner, who was gazing at the hatch, tears streaming down his face.

"He hated me," Donner said brokenly. "But I didn't hate him — I loved him, and pitied him, and I promised our dying mother that I would try to save him. I did try, but it was no use. From the beginning he was wild, reckless, cruel. After our father died he became utterly ruthless. When you rode out of town tonight, I knew you were on his trail. I followed you, hoping against hope to save him from himself. Instead, I sent him to his death."

"Which was the kindest and most merciful thing you could do," Slade said, his voice gentle, his eyes all kindness. "Why did he hate you, Rance?"

"Because I'm tall and straight and not deformed," Donner answered. "He hated all tall, straight men. He hated you the moment he laid eyes on you. Yes, that was the keynote of his life — hate!"

"He had much to bear," Slade said. "Now he's gone to where no doubt crooked bodies are made straight. And souls, too," he added.

"I hope so," said Donner. "Anyhow, it makes me feel better to hear you say it." He turned, walked to the rail and stood gazing across the dark water, lifted his eyes to the stars, drew a deep breath, turned back to Slade and managed a wan smile.

"Thank you for everything," he said. "Could — could we get his body up and give it a decent burial?"

"Yes, we'll do that," Slade answered. "And I want to thank you for being alive." Donner bowed his head.

"At least, I saved my brother from having one more terrible sin on his soul, which is something."

"Which is a great deal," Slade corrected. He turned to learn how the posse had made out, and was thankful to learn that nobody had been killed. Sheriff Cole was swabbing blood from a gashed cheek. Clark had a bullet scrape along his ribs, which he was examining to the accompaniment of vivid profanity. Cock Badding had lost part of a finger, which he made light of. "A plumb fine wring," he chortled, his eyes shining. "Ain't had so much fun since Pop got drunk and fell down the well."

Two deputies had suffered minor wounds. Slade's own throat was sore and swollen, but that would soon mend.

"What about the ship?" asked Cole.

"Leave it here with a couple of the boys to keep an eye on it," Slade decided. "It's Donner's property now, I suppose. The captain and his mate will accompany us to Corpus Christi, under guard. They'll have a little explaining to do to the Customs people, and you should be able to make some sort of a case against them. I don't see any sense in taking the sailors into custody. They are in the nature of hired hands who obey orders, and somebody will be needed to look after the ship. Commandeer one of the wagons and load the prisoners and the bodies into it. The other horses can be led."

All of which was speedily taken care of. Hayes Wilfred's body had been retrieved from the hold and was also placed in the wagon.

"Wilfred was my father's name, John Wilfred Donner," Rance Donner replied to a question from Slade. "Our mother's maiden name was Hayes and is my middle name. My brother was named Hayes Wilfred Donner. He repudiated the name of Donner after our father died, and followed me to Corpus Christi when I moved there after the big hurricane. I don't know, but I fear he was always looking for a chance to kill me. He started stories about me that didn't do me any good, nearly wrecked several of my ships — I let him take the best of the fleet and took the old tubs — had my sailors assaulted by the Border ruffians he hired for such chores and to help in the smuggling. He set fire to the Cambria that night, and she would have burned if it hadn't been for you and Norton. I suppose I should have reported him," he added wearily, "but I just couldn't do it. I always hoped he would eventually straighten out. He never did."

"All of which is just as you figured it, Slade," interpolated Sheriff Cole. "Well, I guess everything ended for the best and maybe we'll have a mite of peace, and perhaps no Border row, for a while."

Clark Kendal insisted that a stopover be made at the Tumbling K ranch for a snack and a mite of rest, a suggestion everybody was glad to accept.

"And now what about you?" he asked Slade.

"I'll have to ride on to town," Slade said. "Tomorrow or the day after I hope to be back with you for a day or two. Then I'll be heading for the Post. Captain Jim will very likely have some other little chore lined up for me by the time I get there."

Slade spent two very pleasant days and nights, at the Tumbling K. He hated to tear himself away from his affable host and his charming hostess, but felt he had no choice in the matter; Captain Jim might be needing him.

Kendal, Gay and old Peterby were the last to bid him farewell. Kendal shook hands with warmth before he swung into the saddle. Gay's eyes were misty.

"You'll be back?" she asked.

"Yes, I'll be back, soon I hope," Slade replied and kissed her goodbye, old Clark smiling his approval.

They watched him ride away, tall and graceful atop his great black horse, the rays of the low-lying sun etching his sternly handsome profile in flame. Old Peterby spoke.

"Folks," he said solemnly, "there goes a *man!*"